I'll Be Strong for You

I'll Be Strong for You

A NOVEL

Nasim Marashi

Translated from the Persian by Poupeh Missaghi

ASTRA HOUSE | NEW YORK

Originally published in the Persian language as
Payiz fasl-e akhar-e sal ast by Nasim Marashi.

Astra House
A Division of Astra Publishing House
astrahouse.com
Printed in the United States of America

Publisher's Cataloging-in-Publication Data
Names: Mar'ashī, Nasīm, 1984-, author. | Missaghi, Poupeh, translator.
Title: I'll be strong for you : a novel / Nasim Marashi ; translated from the Persian by Poupeh Missaghi.
Description: Originally published in the Persian language as Payiz fasl-e akhar-e sal ast. | New York, NY: Astra House, A Division of Astra Publishing House, 2021.
Identifiers: ISBN 978-1-6626-0036-4 (hardcover) | 978-1-6626-0037-1 (ebook) | 978-1-6626-0038-8 (trade audio) | 978-1-6626-0041-8 (library audio)
Subjects: LCSH Women—Iran—Fiction. | Friendship—Fiction. | Persian fiction—Women authors— Translations into English. | Persian fiction—20th century—Translations into English. | BISAC FICTION / Cultural Heritage | FICTION / Contemporary Women
Classification: LCC PK6562.23.A737213 I55 2021 | DDC 891.553—dc23

First edition
10 9 8 7 6 5 4 3 2 1

Design by Richard Oriolo
The text is set in Bulmer MT Std.
The titles are set in Mostra Nuova AltC.

For Felicetta Ferraro, who was eternally hopeful

Contents

I'll Be Strong for You

Summer

ONE

I WAS RUNNING AFTER YOU. Over the cold white tiles of the boarding area. In the haunting thousand-year-old silence. My panting grew louder in my ears with every step, turning the taste in my throat bitter. The international flights area was on the other side. It wasn't the Imam Khomeini Airport; it looked more like Mehrabad. The boarding area kept moving farther and farther away, but somehow I arrived at the gate. You had your back to me, but I recognized you. You were wearing your light blue coat and you stood there, holding on to your carry-on, waiting calmly. The light was blindingly white. I could only see the light and you. A light blue spot in absolute white. I called your name. You began to walk away, gaining distance. You were sliding over the floor tiles. I ran, reached out my hand, and grabbed yours. Your hand remained in mine, and the airplane took off.

I'm still at the threshold of dreams, that painful threshold between sleeping and staying awake that traps an endless yawn in my cells. I've forced my eyes all the way open to end this suffering. I notice the half-open door of the closet in front of me and the unlit lamp on a nightstand full of dirty glasses, a broken clock, and some books. Your books. I run my hand over the sheet next to me. You're not there. No one is there. Where am I? How old am I? What day is it? I don't know. The only thing I know is I'm not feeling well. I taste the bitterness deep in my throat and something is fluttering in my heart. I'm thirsty. I have to remember. I pull my left hand out from under my body. The stainless steel watch has left marks on my sweaty wrist. Eleven fifteen. When did it get so late? I close my eyes and squeeze my head in my hands. I think about yesterday, the day before yesterday. I remember it's Sunday and I have a meeting. I throw the blanket to the side.

When I picked up the phone, he had said, "Hello, Ms. Leyla. I'm Amir Salehi. Saghar gave me your number."

He had said they were starting a newspaper. That they are going to publish three arts and culture pages every day. One page goes to print around noon, the other two in the evening. He had said if I had the time and was interested, I should stop by the office Sunday afternoon.

I do have time. As much time as he wants. In the past four months, I haven't had anything except for useless time. Wasted time, time that is not of my life, that doesn't take anything from it or add anything to it. I didn't get along with the editor in chief of the weekly I was working for. Four months ago, he had stood in front of me and said, "Your article belongs to me, and I can do whatever I want with it." I gathered my papers. He asked, "How great do you think your writing is that no one is allowed to change a single word?" I threw my books and pens in my purse. He said, "I don't want to hear about you making a complaint ever again." I threw my purse on my shoulder and said, "You won't, ever again," and walked out. He didn't understand that the change he had made had ruined my article. Since the day I quit, I wake up every morning, trace the sun as it moves across the sky, step by step, until it is night, when I fall asleep. I don't remember doing anything else. Sometimes I see Roja or Shabaneh—they come over or we go out to grab a bite, and then I come back home again. Once Dad came too, and we traveled together to Ahwaz to see Mom and the rest of the family. For three or four days, I don't remember exactly. I do have time for work. As much as he wants. But I don't know if I want to work or not. I should. I probably do want to. I used to like my job. You should know that well—we used to laugh together at work. I remember my laughter. But now, what do I like to do other than lying down and counting the days I have left? I don't know.

Dad said, "Let me get you a job at the National Oil Company. You could work in your own field. Earn good money. Build your future. And you'll be close to us as well."

I don't want to go back to Ahwaz. Best to not look back. During my last visit, I realized I couldn't. Ahwaz is hot. The heat rises from the ground and crashes on your chest. How many times can you walk to the sea and back, when it only takes twenty minutes? How long can you sit under the air conditioner that brings in a nice earthy smell, reading a magazine? How often can you go to Kian Bazaar and bargain with the Arab women over dates and pomfret fish and laugh? This time when I went back home, Ahwaz seemed smaller. Smaller than what it was during my childhood. I could cross any street by taking only four steps. Chahar Shir was now connected to Palm Square, Palm Square to Seyed Khalaf. The courtyards were small and the trenches left from the war as tiny as matchboxes. When I stared at them, they disturbed the images of my childhood, confusing my memories. I couldn't relax there at night. I wanted my own house. My own bed. Our own bed.

Shabaneh said, "Come join our company. They're hiring. We'll all be together, like in college. It'll be fun."

It won't be fun, I know that. I will have to sit at a desk every day and write numbers on paper, on plans, on the monitor. The fours will combine with the twos, the twos with the fives, and the numbers will line up one after the other and chew my brain. They will have minuses and decimal points. Zero, dot, three. Zero, dot, eight. The diameter of the shaft multiplied by the height of the vane, the length of the piston minus the size of the cylinder decreased from the size of the cylinder, and all this will drive me crazy. Like in college, Shabaneh will turn inward, and Roja will disappear behind her computer. Nobody will talk to me. I will be left all alone in that gloomy office.

Roja said, "Let's pack everything and go. You just have to pass the language test. I'll take care of admissions and visas. Why do you want to stay here?"

"If I wanted to leave, I would've left with Misagh."

"You're being stubborn, Leyla. Stop doing this to yourself."

I don't want to leave. Why doesn't anyone understand what I say? And now, even if I wanted to, I don't have the energy anymore. I don't have Roja's energy or yours. I've witnessed what it means to leave with my own eyes. You were there in my own house, and each and every form and paper that you prepared became a step in a ladder taking you farther and farther away from me. It was a hard process. You put together hundreds of letters and documents. You had them translated, notarized, and signed, and you made an appointment at the embassy . . . Appointment at the embassy? Today is Sunday. Roja had an appointment at the embassy early this morning. I told her I would wake her up. Why did I forget?

"The person you are trying to reach is currently . . ."

She must have gotten up on time and left for the embassy already; that's why her phone is turned off. Roja is not someone to miss her appointments. She is strong, like you.

I feel lightheaded. I have to make tea and eat something. The moment I step out of the room, the chaos of the apartment overwhelms me. The ashtray is full of cigarette butts. You hated that and would keep emptying it, saying that the apartment would smell like a dorm if you didn't. The kitchen counter is crowded with dirty napkins and dishes soiled with the congealed grease of half-eaten food. The glass tabletop is smudged in dirty fingerprints, yesterday's newspapers and the ones from the day before and the past week stacked high and unread. My manteau is abandoned on the couch. I go back to the bedroom and hide under the blanket. This is not my home. I have to capture the day that is escaping me and make this a home again. If I go back to work and feel better and continue to feel better, I'll take care of the apartment again. I'll organize everything. I'll change the broken light bulbs. I'll have my red furniture set repaired—the fabric is dirty and the springs are broken. It needs to be polished and a couple of white buttons replaced to make it look like new. You didn't like the set. You'd grown tired of the color. You'd said you would, from the first day, from the day we went shopping for it. You and I, along with Roja and Shabaneh, skipped our noon class and left campus. Mom had not yet come to help us out. We were going to visit furniture stores around Tehran to pick a set so we wouldn't have to drag her all over the city. Roja suggested going to Yaft Abad. I didn't feel like going all the way there. She said it would be just one trip, but I knew she would want to take me to the other side of town a hundred times just for a few pieces of furniture. You suggested we let Roja do whatever she liked, and Shabaneh, as always, looked at us and didn't say a word. As we were passing the Jahan Koodak intersection, I noticed a big store and a red set in the window. I fell in love with its white buttons and large flowers. You said, "Red furniture? You'll grow tired of it after a few days. Look at the beige and brown ones. See how beautiful they are . . ."

Roja frowned. "How old are you two? Now is the time to buy red furniture. When you grow old, you can go sit contentedly on those ugly brown ones and hug your grandchildren."

I loved the red set. I wouldn't grow tired of it, I was sure. I looked at Shabaneh. She didn't have an opinion.

"Both the red ones and the brown ones are beautiful. Don't you want to go check Yaft Abad as well?"

I didn't want to go to Yaft Abad. I just wanted those. The red ones that were expensive and too bright and would make our home happy. Like us. I called Dad.

"Don't think about the price, my darling. You will be using them for many years. You should buy whatever color you like. Whatever you want."

I did buy them. You weren't unhappy with them. You passed your hand over the flowers and said they were soft. When Mom arrived, we went and bought brown curtains so that the decor would suit both my taste and yours. It's been seven years, and the curtains are old now. I have to change them. If I start working again and feel better, I'll sit down and decide which color fits the red better than the brown and change the curtains. I'll make the apartment beautiful again. When I feel better again.

I want tea. I try not to look around at the living room and instead walk straight to the kitchen. I pick up the kettle, which is covered with multicolored stains, its heaviness reminding me of the descaler I keep forgetting to buy. I fill it up and put it on the stove next to all the dried yellow and red grease stains, crispy rice grains, and pasta pieces caked with sauce. I stare at the dirty fingerprints on the fridge door; at the cabinets full of bread crumbs and empty plastic bags; at the dried yogurt stain, which turns my stomach with its ugly, cracked, desertlike yellow. I can smell the dirty dishes left in the sink for several days. I should ask Ms. Molouk to come wash them. I've been meaning to call her for several months, but I don't have the patience to watch over her all day long and listen to the stories of her poor divorced daughter and her disabled sister-in-law who has been a burden for the past twenty years. I wish Mom would come and spread good cheer in the home. She would bring Ms. Molouk, fill up the freezer, fill the apartment with the scent of her cooking, and sit and talk and talk. She would tell me about my auntie who bought a new car; of my uncle's wife who hasn't called for some time to ask after Grandpa; of Dad, who misses Samira and me, and who, every night when he gets home from his work, wishes his two daughters would be there for dinner with him; of her cousin and how she is handling her twins; and of the new Persian words Samira's kid has learned and how beautifully he pronounces them. I would just sit across from her on the couch, drink the freshly brewed, beautifully colored tea, eat peeled oranges, and listen to her voice echoing throughout the apartment and just tut-tut in response for no good reason.

I pour the hot water into my tea glass and the brown clouds spread out and swirl into the water. I bob the tea bag. The clouds mix with one another and make instant tea for me. You are not here anymore, and I have, with no regrets, put the teapot away in the upper cabinet. I only use tea bags now. I have to drink tea to feel fresh. I have to go to work feeling fresh. I'll go back to the job that I've always loved, the job that used to make me happy. I'll have to learn to love it once again. Why don't I? Why does nothing make me laugh anymore these days? Perhaps it's unemployment. I need something to lose myself in so that I don't feel where I am. I have to pass my days somehow. Something to distract me from everything. Right now, nothing distracts me; thoughts just keep sneaking around. When I sprawl myself out on the red couch, I don't feel bored—even if I sit there for thousands of hours. So many thoughts rush into my head—about myself, you, Samira, Shabaneh, and Mahan. Thoughts about how we ended up here; where we went wrong; where in our origin story and with what force did our foundation crack so deep that, without even realizing it and with just one breeze, we crumbled down on top of ourselves, unable to get back on our feet? We can't shake ourselves and stand up again, and even if we could, we are not what we used to be before the collapse. Which engineer made a mistake in computing our forces, building our structure in such an unstable way that it could break down at any moment? The thought of a life without laughter and dreams shatters me into pieces, like the ugly yellow yogurt stain on the kitchen counter. But if I have a job, I'll stop thinking. I'll work until I'm exhausted, and then I'll hold my exhaustion in my arms and gradually go to sleep. Roja said, "Why are you so hard on yourself? You don't need to work." Why couldn't she understand that this was the only solace in my fucking life? The only one. Since you left, nothing else remains. But I have to be happy now. I have to remember my happiness. I squeeze my head in my hands and search for the sound of my own loud laughter.

"Come on, Leyli. Stop dawdling. We're going to be late."

"Please. Just give me a second. I can't rush."

My hand was in yours and I was laughing out loud. I was bent over, on the side of the street. I couldn't breathe and still remember the pain in my stomach from laughing so hard. You pulled my arm. We were late. What were we laughing at? I don't remember. I just remember we were in Enghelab Avenue. Bahman Cinema. We had just watched a bad movie in the Fajr film festival and were heading back to campus. On Kargar Avenue, between the CD street peddlers, sambusa stands, cheap print shops, thrift stores, and Fooman cookie sellers, we were looking for a cab, passing through the crowd of arms and shoulders and waists. You were wearing the white shirt Samira had sent you. A man was rushing in our direction with his head down. You let go of my arm to let him pass. I laughed again, and the man looked up at me. You hesitated for a second and stepped toward me. When the man brought his head up, it was already too late. His head bumped into your chest, and the pomegranate juice in his cup sloshed on your white shirt. It left a stain that never disappeared as long as you were here with me. It did not come out with baking powder, nor with vinegar, nor bleach, nor the Rafuneh's stain remover I used the last time I washed it before I put it in your suitcase. I said, "Only wear it in the house, when no one is around."

My tea is already cold, and I swallow it in one gulp. I am surprised by the sound. Is it the silence of the apartment that makes the sound of my swallowing reverberate so loudly in my head? Or is it that my ears are not used to hearing things anymore? I've gotten used to the silence of the empty home, the stifling air, and the imprisonment behind the double-paned, soundproof windows. I don't even want to play the piano anymore. How long has it been since I last played? Four months? Eight? I don't remember. I open my fingers wide, clench them into a fist, open them wide again. I feel the pain all the way up to my wrists. My fingers are not soft and weightless anymore.

They've become short and ugly; the knuckles have become thick and stiff, pained by any extra movement. With this pain and these long misshapen nails that scrape on the piano keys, I can no longer play the section from Waltz in A Minor that you liked. You came and sat next to me on the piano bench and said, "I like it that you always keep your nails short and never wear nail polish."

I explained to you that it was because of the piano and taught you to play the bass E minor octave at the beginning of every beat while I played Chopin. You said, "I fell in love with you that very day. The day you sat at the piano in the auditorium and, I believe, played a piece by Chopin. Did you know I was watching you?"

"Were you really watching me? I thought I was the one who first fell in love with you, on that day during the strike when you were sitting on the top step of the student union office, wearing a velvet French beret, more confident than all the others."

"I still love to watch your fingers dancing on the instrument when you play, unaware of your surroundings."

Whenever I practiced, I knew you were standing in the doorway, watching me. How can I play now that you are not here to watch me? You are not here, and my fingers have forgotten how to dance. They've become stiff, and I don't remember anything of Chopin anymore. I have to fix things. When I go back to work and recapture the good days that are now escaping me, I'll have the piano tuned. I'll practice again until my fingers go back to how they were before you left. I have to find my sheet music.

Why is today just dragging on and on? It's not even one o'clock yet. I turn on my laptop and open my email, hoping for the one message that is never there. "Important, Important, Important." "Three Methods to Prevent Breast Cancer." "Beautiful Iranian Model in New York City." I delete them all, close my tabs, and go to my blog.

My post from yesterday has eleven comments. I'd written about my new job offer, about Salehi, the newspaper, and the good days that are to come, the simplest preoccupations in the world. The comments read, "Congratulations." "When are you treating us to something?!" "Finally, you wrote something." "Check out our page too," and other similar notes. I like that I don't have to see these people face to face. I like that whenever I want to say something, I can say it from far away and then hide and only hear their responses on my own time, at a distance. I don't want anyone to sit in front of me and look at me and wait for a response; that's why I like newspapers. I like sitting in the newsroom and writing, then, the following day, standing by the large plane tree in the alley in front of the newsstand to see how many people pause to read the headline of my piece while browsing the paper.

The phone rings. It's Roja. She says she's done at the embassy. "When do you have to be at work?" "Four thirty." I say, and add, "I lay there awake until the sun came up but forgot to wake you up. Did you get there in time?"

She had. "Let's go have lunch." It's only one thirty, and I still have time to kill before my meeting at the newspaper. "Coming?" she asks. "I'm not in the mood to go to work now. We'll have lunch, then I'll go to work, and you'll head to the newspaper office."

Something is holding me back. I tell her I am not sure what to do.

"What do you mean you're not sure? Come on, let's go. I don't have a car. I'll meet you at a quarter past two, at the intersection of Apadana and Niloufar. We'll walk somewhere together. You'll come, right? If you remain silent, it means you agree."

If I remain silent, it means I agree? No, I don't. When I agree with something, I am not silent. I laugh. I open my mouth and say, "Yes, I agree." But silence . . . I know I don't remain silent. Maybe I had remained silent that day too, and you had assumed that I was agreeing. I sat in silence and packed your suitcase. I was not agreeing with you leaving; I was just silent, and then you left without me. Before leaving, you went to see your parents. Perhaps you laughed a lot and joked with your mother and asked her not to miss you too much. Perhaps you embraced and kissed your aunts who had come to see you before you left and told them you would be back soon. I opened your suitcase two or three times to make sure you weren't leaving anything behind and closed it again, remaining silent all along. You wandered through the city with friends and said your goodbyes. Perhaps you urged them to keep me company and to take good care of me when you were gone. I remained silent and zipped your suitcase one last time, and perhaps you joked around and smiled with hope at everyone you were leaving behind. I locked your suitcase. You opened the apartment door and came in. I was silent, but I am sure I was not in agreement. I thought that you wouldn't leave. I was waiting for you to come into the room, kiss me, and say, "I've changed my mind. I won't go anywhere if you don't support my decision." I was waiting for you to come in and say, "Of course I won't leave you. Where can I go without you?" I was certain you wouldn't leave. Even when you called a cab and said you were headed to Imam Khomeini, I thought to myself that you wouldn't leave without me. I stood in the doorway. You changed, and I looked away. You wore your new shirt and sweater. I had taken the tags off and put them on the bed. I had bought them myself for your trip, to make sure you would be the most elegant passenger on your flight. A lilac-striped shirt, a gray sweater, and a dark pair of jeans. Your light blue coat was on the bed too. You unzipped your backpack to put in the clothes you had just taken off.

"I've packed new clothes for you. Don't take these."

You said okay. You didn't look at me. You grabbed your socks. I went and sat down on the couch in the living room and picked up my book. I had to stop myself from crying. You wouldn't leave. I was sure you wouldn't leave without me. You wanted to scare me. I heard the suitcase wheels. You were standing by the front door, and I looked at you over the top of my book. You were wearing your light blue coat. You put your backpack on the floor, put on your shoes, and tied the laces slowly. When you looked in my direction, I looked down.

"Come into my arms."

I didn't. I went to our bedroom and closed the door. Your clothes were on the bed—the only bright presence of yours to remain in the house after you. I listened until I heard the sound of the front door opening and closing and the sound of the suitcase wheels moving away. I had to stop myself from crying. You would come back. I was sure of it. You could not leave without me and live and be happy. You would come back very soon. Perhaps from the airport. Perhaps tomorrow or the day after.

Out of all my clothes, I pick a dark pair of jeans and a gray manteau to wear. Can you see me? I look like you did when you were headed toward your new life. Now I'm the one heading toward my new life, and looking like you will bring me luck. I check out my face in the mirror. How many days has it been since I wore makeup? My eyes look so clean. I empty my bag on the bed in search of my eyeliner. I pull the corner of my left eye to unwrinkle the skin and draw a black line above my eyelashes. It goes wrong, like always, like all the lines in my life that I've drawn that went wrong, that I erased and drew again only to have them go wrong again. Like the hundred dashes I drew with a red pencil in between the words for "father" in black ink as we did our nightly homework drills, all of which went wrong, so I erased them and drew them once more and they went wrong again, leaving me with nothing but ripped-apart pages. I would beg Samira to draw the dashes for me. She wouldn't. "You're crazy. These are fine!" she said. And with eyes full of tears, I would keep erasing and drawing. But I don't have any energy left to erase now. I just draw another line on top of it, make it thicker so that its twistedness gets lost in the black of the eyeliner.

All my scarves are piled up on top of one another in the closet. Plain black, checkered blue, beige with orange flowers, a two-tone purple-and-brown one, and again plain black. One is ugly, the other wrinkled. I pull the purple one out. I haven't worn it since I bought it with Roja a few months ago. It has remained all new for this very day.

"Buy it. You're light-skinned. Purple suits you. You should get used to wearing bright colors."

I should get used to wearing bright colors, to being happy and energetic. I am starting a new job. A profession I've loved forever. I open the drawer under the vanity mirror looking for a cheerful lipstick. I still have one. It is dark pink and smells old. I put it on. I look ugly. I wipe it off. The color that remains will do. I'm not going to a party.

The black Peugeot that's usually parked in front of my car is not there today, and I can easily get out of my spot. Perhaps today is going to be a good day. I turn onto the highway and get stuck in the mass of cars and sweaty drivers and horns and the heavy air invading me. Traffic shouldn't be this heavy at lunchtime. Why doesn't it want to be a good day? The car doesn't work properly, and my feet don't sit right on the gas and brake pedals. How long has it been since I last drove? I turn the AC on. The fan cools my neck, but the seat feels odd under my body. I move around, adjust my manteau underneath me. I move the seat forward, push the back down, unbuckle the seat belt . . . it's no use. I roll down my window to let some air in. It is hot, hot and polluted. The settled heat of the month of Mordad is different from the fresh heat of Khordad. The heat of Khordad is new, and its sun is clean. It pours light all over you. But Mordad is so filthy, greasy, and musty that even its sun rays pass through a lot of dirt before latching onto your body, and there is no way to get rid of its dead, stifling smell. I want to turn around and go back home right now, sit under the cool water drops in the shower, lean my head on the wall, and listen to the sound of cold water dropping on the blue tiles. A car behind me honks, and something thumps inside my chest. There is no air. I feel like I'm suffocating. In my purse, my fingers brush over my phone and wallet and headphones and pen and dried cigarette packs and a notebook until I find my pack of Librium. The green pill is tiny and slippery, easy to swallow without water.

"You are stressed, my darling. Try not to put yourself in stressful situations. Whenever you feel palpitations, take one. It won't make you sleepy, and you won't get addicted. Just don't overdo it."

The palpitations had started a while ago. At inconvenient times, my heart would pound heavily on the walls of my chest, and something would flow from it all through my body. Then it would beat fast, so fast that it made me short of breath. I was afraid I would have a heart attack in my sleep, wake up suffocating, panting so hard I'd turn blue and die, alone. Nobody would find me for several days, and I would rot away and begin to smell. I felt ashamed, thinking of the people who would break into the apartment, covering their mouths with white handkerchiefs against the foul smell of my blue corpse. I made an appointment with Dad's old classmate. He did an ECG and an echo, and then called Dad.

"There's no problem with her heart."

Dad told him to prescribe me some Librium. His friend handed me the phone to talk to him.

"Take one whenever you feel distressed. Do you want to come stay with us for a while?"

"No."

"Do you want me or Mom to come to Tehran and stay with you for a few days? Do you want me to tell Samira to send you a letter of invitation so you can go to France and stay with her for a while?"

I didn't want to. I didn't have it in me to go. Neither to Ahwaz nor to France. Nor anywhere else. I just wanted my bed. Our bed. Like now. I don't have it in me to fight against all these cars. I wish a large hand would drop down and pick me up and take me to the middle of the winter, on a dead-end street, under the shade of a large pine tree. I wish I could just ram into the car in front of me and push the accelerator hard enough to tear through the cars and crush them one by one to pass through.

I turn onto Niloufar Street. I pass the chocolate shop, the sandwich shop, the doner kebab store, the fast-food store, the toy store, and the police station, then reach Roja, who's waiting for me at the corner, talking on her phone. I call out to her and she turns around. She has dyed her hair red. It looks good on her with the dark green of her eyes. She gets in the car and says goodbye on her phone.

"Your hair looks amazing. It looks good on you."

She runs her hand through her hair.

"I did it yesterday to look nice for the embassy appointment. I like the color, too. How are you?"

"The same. How did the appointment go?"

"They took my documents and said it could be anywhere from three weeks to three months before I hear back."

"So is it three weeks or three months?"

"I'm not sure. They didn't specify."

She rolls the window down and loosens her scarf.

"I'm super hungry. Where should we eat?"

"Wherever. It doesn't matter."

"What do you mean it doesn't matter? You're such a killjoy with this ennui of yours. Shall we go to Bandar? With your parking permit, we should be fine."

Bandar is close by, so I turn onto Mahnaz Street. Roja takes a few DVDs out of her purse and puts them on the back seat.

"Watch these. They're good. I picked them out from dozens, just for you."

"Thanks. Any news from Shabaneh?"

"She's doing fine. After your meeting at the newspaper, you should stop by our office to see her."

"I don't know how long I'll be. Are things okay between her and Arsalan?"

"One day they are and the next day they aren't. He's not a bad guy. Shabaneh had to pick someone eventually. Why aren't you wearing any makeup?"

"I am . . . Can't you tell?"

"Are you serious? It's your first day at work. You should've at least put on some blush to not look like a corpse. You'll scare people away."

"There's nowhere to park here. Where should we park?"

"Just park in front of this gate. We'll keep an eye on the car."

"We can't. We'll block their driveway."

"Just park! I'll worry about the rest."

I get out of the car. I know she'll take care of the rest. She always has the best solutions for taking care of "the rest" of everything. During our fourth semester in college, I fell head over heels for

Misagh, who couldn't stay put and made me feel like he wanted me one day and like he didn't the next. When Roja decided to join the school camping trip in Tabriz, she said, "You just come along. Be a good girl, and I'll take care of the rest." By the time we got back from the trip, I was Misagh's girlfriend, and the following year we were living together.

Roja takes a pen and paper from her purse and writes, "We are at the restaurant." Underneath, she draws a smiley face, and next to it, a big sandwich full of lettuce, and puts the note under the windshield wiper. She grabs my arm and drags me into the sandwich shop. It's cool and crowded, and there is nowhere to sit. Roja walks up to a table for four and sits down even though a guy is already there, busy eating.

"Excuse me, is it okay if we share the table with you?"

I tug at her arm and whisper that I'm not comfortable sharing the table. She points to the man's food.

"He'll be leaving soon. Look, he's almost done."

She drops her purse and papers on the table, next to the man's half-eaten pizza.

"What do you want to eat? Oh, I forgot, you don't care. I'll order you something myself."

She walks to the counter. I don't feel comfortable sitting next to the stranger. I get up and stand next to Roja, who has her hand on the counter and orders half the options on the menu with such precision, it's as if she's solving some component design calculations. When she notices me, she says, "Why did you get up? All my things are back at the table. Didn't you see?"

She pays, and we walk back to the table and sit. I feel uncomfortable but collect myself on the seat. The man is uncomfortable too. Irritated, he gets up and walks away, leaving his food unfinished.

"Poor guy. He was eating. We made him uncomfortable."

"He should have been happy that we sat at his table."

She turns to the waiter, tilting her head and pointing to her belly. Then she pushes her stuff to the side and turns to me. "Why do you look so wiped out again today? Aren't you headed to a new job? All your problems are solved now."

"Was my problem not having a job?"

"Yes, it was. Didn't you keep saying you only had one joy in life? What's the problem now?"

The waiter brings our appetizers. Roja puts a potato salad in front of me.

"Eat. You'll feel better."

When did I ever feel better by eating potato salad? I check my watch. I don't have much time left before my meeting at the newspaper, but my enthusiasm has already dwindled. I wish I could postpone it until tomorrow and just sit here all day.

Roja says, "When you picked me up, I was talking to Samira. She said her husband is going to defend his dissertation in two or three months, and then they'll be visiting Iran together for a few weeks."

"Hopefully she's back in France when you get there so you're not all by yourself."

"I should get used to being all by myself. At the embassy today, they asked me to provide an affidavit of support from someone testifying that they'll put me up for a while. I asked Samira, and she said she would write the letter. It'll be hard for her. She has so much work, a husband, a little baby. It will be a burden for her."

"Don't worry. Samira loves to help out. Also, my mom has already set aside some spices from Abadan, saffron, and frozen herbs for you to take for her. So leave room in your suitcase."

The waiter puts a lasagna in front of me and a pizza in front of Roja. Roja puts both dishes in the middle of the table, next to each other. She takes a bite from one and then from the other. You loved the way she ate. You said watching her eat made you crave food, even if you were completely full. Why can't I keep you out of my mind today? "Do you remember Misagh used to call me Leyli?"

My heart begins to beat a thousand times per minute. It is one thing to just think about you all the time and another to speak of you out loud. When I speak of you, you become real. You become a wave in the air, and everyone sees you. Roja has heard what I said, and once again I share with her the joy of remembering you and the fact that you called me a name no one else did. You would put on your round steel glasses, look at me over the top of your book, and say, "Leyli means the beloved, embodied in the eyes of the lover. It means the purity of love, transcending the beloved. Leyli is the goblet, and love is the wine within. One should hold the goblet and get drunk with the wine."

"Yes. He used to call you Leyli. That's more romantic than Leyla. But why are you thinking of Misagh?

"I dreamed of him last night."

"I sensed that something was wrong with you today. Please, don't think about him—just for today. Eat. Today is an important day. You should have good thoughts."

Something squeezes my heart. She's right. Thinking about you has stopped being a good thing for a long while now. What difference does it make whether you called me Leyli or Leyla? What difference does it make that the furniture of our house was red instead of brown? That you wore your light blue coat instead of the dark blue one? That you liked the way Roja ate or not? What matters is that you shouldn't have left, but you did. I should not be thinking of you on such an important day.

"You've made a habit of feeling sad, Leyla. You've turned your life into a wake—all you are missing is some chest-beating mourners. Go ahead and dig a grave for Misagh and cry over it day in, day out, but don't turn the rest of the world into a graveyard too. Eat your food."

I run my hand over my throat. The hard lump is back, blocking everything. The lump that has been in my throat since the day you left. No doctor's prescription has had any effect on it. I took some pills for two months, then had some injections, and grew weaker by the day. Until Dad came to Tehran. But even he failed to see the lump.

"It won't heal, Dad. There is no way it can heal."

"Your throat is completely healthy, my darling. Who prescribed antibiotics for you?"

Roja puts her hands on her belly and calls the waiter.

"Can you please give us some to-go boxes? We'll take the rest home."

I give her a look. She bristles at me.

"Don't be so bougie. You didn't eat anything, so what do you care anyway? I'll take it to Shabaneh."

She takes her phone out of her purse and makes a call.

"Hi, Shabaneh. What's up at the office? . . . My appointment took longer than I expected. I just had lunch with Leyla . . . Pizza and lasagna. I'm bringing you some lasagna . . . Okay."

She hands me the phone.

"What's up, Shabaneh?"

"Nothing. I mean, I'll tell you later. Was lunch good?"

"Yes, not bad. Do you want anything?"

"A sandwich."

"I'll tell Roja to get you one. What kind?"

"You know what, I don't want anything. Don't worry about it. We'll go grab something together some other time."

"Are you sure?"

"Yes. I'll call you tonight. I need to talk to you."

"I'll be waiting for your call."

Roja gets up. I hang up and say, "Let's go together, Roja. I'll give you a ride."

"Are you crazy? In this traffic, if you drop me off and go back, you'll be late for work. I'll just get a cab around the corner."

"But how long could it possibly take?"

"A long time. You'll have a hard time on the way back. Instead of giving me a lift, just walk to your office from here. Do some window-shopping, watch the crowds and the busy streets. Buy yourself something. It will do you good. Haft-e Tir Square is close by. Don't you need anything?"

Don't I need anything? I do—scarves, manteaus, shirts, pants, everything. All my clothes are old now. Mom said, "Not even Ms. Molouk's kid dresses like you do. Do you want me to ask Samira to buy you some clothes and mail them to you?" I didn't want her to ask. But now that I'm going to work and I'm supposed to feel better, I can just go and buy everything I need and head to work with several bags of new clothes, like a regular happy twenty-eight-year-old. Then I can tell everyone that I was passing Haft-e Tir Square, saw these clothes, liked them, and bought them for myself.

Roja says goodbye and runs with her purse and papers in hand toward Motahhari Avenue. There is now an empty parking spot in front of my car. I move it there. I can wander around until four and then head to the office. I walk toward the shops, and the crowds and busy streets make me feel better. I walk down the street and make a right. Then I walk along Mofatteh Alley all the way to Haft-e Tir. Every time I make a turn, the number of people grows, and they walk faster and faster, and like fluid molecules with Brownian motion, they bump into one another and pass by one another. The sidewalk and the street, the spaces between the large buses and small cars, are all filled with people who talk with one another or on their phones. Their lips move as if in a nightmare, and they speak strange words in a language I don't know. There are thousands of people. They all seem to be speaking in my head. The heat is driving me crazy. The loud horn of a bus startles me. Someone bumps into me. I step aside and find refuge in a cool, uncrowded store. When I catch my breath in the cool air of the AC, I look up and see a wall of colorful socks. The shelves behind the saleswoman are full of scarves, and, under the glass counter, there is an assortment of glittery hair clips. The saleswoman has large lips and breasts and thin eyebrows. Frowning, she is busy fumbling with her phone. I can hear the sound of colorful balls being shot and exploding. She has dyed-blond hair under her black lace scarf. I'm not sure whether I am looking at her breasts or her lips when she puts the phone aside and asks me what I am looking for. Roja said I should buy something. I glance around at the walls and say, "A pair of socks."

"They are behind you. You can just take any pair you want."

My eyes search through the socks, from yellow to blue and from red to black, and I pause on the pink ones. They are decorated with a ribbon and two small white flowers on the top edge. Shabaneh would like them. I put them on the glass counter. "Five thousand tomans," the woman says. When I pay, she puts them in a bright thin plastic bag and goes back to exploding more colorful balls on her phone. I walk out. The weight of the crowd collapses on my chest again. This is enough for today. I'll come back another day to buy everything I need. Another day, when I've started work and feel better. I turn onto the least crowded alley and walk back to my car. The incline makes me short of breath. Roja once said, "It's because you are not active enough."

She walked into the bedroom, took me by the hand, and brought me to the living room. She turned the music up and started to dance. Her colorful body twirled in the air. I stood by the counter and looked at her hands moving up and down. She took my hand and swirled me around the room.

"Dance. Move your hands and twirl. You can't keep living life like this."

I couldn't twirl. The music sounded like guns, mortar shells, sirens, and rockets. Roja held my hand and kept turning around. Her feet shifted back and forth between her toes and her heels. Her arms waved like fish in the air. She shook her head, and her long curly hair fanned out in the air.

"Why are you just standing there? Dance, Leyla. Move a little. Look, your body is as limp as an old woman's."

I couldn't. My brain couldn't process the rhythm of the song. My arms remained hanging, indecisive, in the air, and I kept forgetting which foot had to go on tiptoe. The music was driving me crazy. I sat on the couch and covered my ears.

I get into my car. I am approaching my new office. A new environment with new people. New, fresh, novel. All of it is good. I should be happy. I should think of good things. Maybe of you. When I think of you, my mind doesn't wander around restlessly. Maybe you could be here, sitting next to me, giving me a ride to work. Maybe I had been out of work for a while, and you were going to work in the mornings, and whenever you came home in the evenings, the apartment was clean and dinner ready. Maybe in these months of unemployment I had turned into the woman of the house. Maybe you would say, "Now that you're going back to work, should we order takeout?" And maybe I would laugh and look at you in a way that would imply, "What nonsense is this?" And you would say, "Your cooking was just beginning to get good!" "That's not fair! When did I ever feed you bad food?" Then I would take a deep breath and say, "I'm really worried about this new job. I'm afraid I won't be able to handle it."

You would put my hand on the stick shift, under your own hand. I would look at my hand hidden under your long fingers. You would say, "Don't worry. I'm sure you can handle it."

And add, "I'll make dinner tonight."

My heart would burst with joy. When we would arrive at the office, my fingers would be all sweaty under yours. I would say goodbye in a way that meant I was head over heels in love with you and I would get out of the car with the weightlessness of a bird that has flown from a tree to pick a seed from the ground.

I park the car in front of the office building. Salehi had given me the address. It's a beautiful new building with huge plants in front of its glass doors. It doesn't have a sign yet, but everything else looks like a first-rate newspaper office. A guard sitting on a plastic chair by the door follows me with his eyes. I tell him I have a meeting with Mr. Salehi.

"Please go ahead. First floor, to the left."

I walk upstairs and strain my ears, hoping to hear a familiar voice. The building is quiet, and I can't hear the usual newsroom sounds. To the right, there is a small room where an old man is busy talking on the phone. I don't know him. Two workers are carrying a desk down the stairs. I hold my purse in my arms and step aside to give them space. When they pass, I see an open-plan office to the left that is full of desks. It looks like an apartment whose walls have been removed. If I utter anything, I know my voice is going to echo through the space. Two people sit at one of the desks, and at another, a man appears to be lost among bits of computer hardware strewn across the desk. He is separating entangled colored wires and connecting each to a different port. One corner of the office is partitioned off into a small room, perhaps for interviews or meetings or as one of the editors' offices. I'm wondering if I should say hello. I hear a drilling noise. The man looks up from the wires, and I say, "I'm looking for Mr. Salehi."

I look around. If one of the people there is Salehi, he will look up.

"Please take a seat. That's his desk. He'll be back in a moment."

I walk to the desk at the end of the hall. The sound of my heels on the stone tile floor makes me nervous. I tiptoe the rest of the way to Salehi's desk. I sit and put my purse on my lap. I don't remember whether, in such situations, I used to put my purse on the desk or on my lap or on the floor or hang it on the back of the chair. I have my back to the room, and the empty space behind me is making me anxious. I wish Salehi were here, talking to one of the men—to break the silence. I don't know how much time passes in silence before I hear one of the men saying, "Amir, someone's here to see you."

I turn around. A chubby man with long hair and a beard walks out from behind the partition. He wears a loose white shirt with nastaliq calligraphy on it. He dries his hands with a paper towel, smiles, and says a warm hello, as if he already knows me very well. I get up. Not sure what to do with my purse, I put it on the desk.

"Welcome."

Salehi looks different than I had expected. I imagined him to be a tall, thin man, with glasses, with no beard or mustache, wearing formal men's clothing. He would be serious and not talkative, his hands always in his pockets, giving orders without even glancing at anyone. But this Salehi looks me straight in the eyes and stretches his hand out. It is still damp, and I like that he doesn't really care.

"I've read your writing, both on your blog and in different journals. You write well. Saghar said you're also organized and reliable."

He laughs. Perhaps he is a cheerful person—otherwise, why would he laugh about someone being organized and reliable? I laugh too, and my laughter tells me that I'm happy.

"The team we work with is a good one. Other than Saghar, who else do you know?"

He doesn't wait for my answer.

"It's important to me that the staff be friendly with one another—it makes the work easier. That is, of course, assuming we don't get tangled up in some nonsense."

He laughs again, and I too allow my laughter to find its way deeper into my chest.

"Regarding the workload, I should say that we don't have a big team. Our budget is limited for now. We have two journalists for each desk, and that makes the workload a bit heavy. I thought you would be a good choice for one of the desks that needs to wrap up its pieces before the evening shift. It's culture-related entertainment news for a public audience. Things like which actor has reconciled with which director, how much an author's book has sold, who's spoken against whose Oscar prize, which philosopher has recently married and what he's said about it, things like this that the average reader would want to know."

Happiness leaves the deepest place in my chest and disappears in the air like cigarette smoke. I look at my fingers. One of my nails has chipped. I start to pick at it.

"Some of the articles require original reporting, but most will be translated from foreign sources. Your English is good, right?"

I don't want to hear more. My new job was not supposed to be like this. I wanted to be offered a serious cultural reporting job, an adult job. He should have said that I would need to get exclusive interviews, or write long reported pieces, or write reviews. Being part of the paparazzi reporting on philosophers' weddings was not supposed to be my job. I have picked at my nail, and now it's twisted on the other side. If I try to set it straight, it will dig into my flesh. To hell with it. I won't accept this shitty job.

"I'd better tell you about the financial aspect up front. We've set aside six hundred fifty-thousand tomans a month for the journalists. It's not much, but we'll try to pay on time."

He laughs once again. I turn away from his meaningless laughter—it's making me anxious. What would you think if I told you I've joined a newspaper to write about philosophers and writers getting married? But what would I do with my life if I don't accept? Once again the same dragging days that never turn into nights, once again insomnia, once again the daily calls to Roja and Shabaneh to ask what they're up to later so that I don't have to be alone in the sad evenings. If I accept, maybe I can stay with the team and then get another position. Perhaps they want to see my work first before they offer me to write for another section of the paper. I'm fooling myself. Like a lover who, instead of a kiss, has received a slap in the face and tells herself that if he didn't desire her he wouldn't . . . If they had another position, they would've offered me that. I run my hand over the sharpness of my broken nail, and my heart beats heavily in my chest. I wish I had a nail file in my purse.

When are these detestable situations in my life going to end? These tormenting decisions between bad and worse. Junctures that all lead to a burnt city. The road to failure should be the only road available so that its suffering results only from that failure. There should always be just the one road, so you can simply go all the way to the end without any guilt, without the torture of temptation by the road not taken, which makes every step you take feebler than the previous one. There should always be just the one road. Just the one. A job needs to be either good or bad, so that I can clearly know whether to take it or not.

He says, "So I've covered everything. What do you think?"

I don't have it in me to respond to his laughter with more laughter.

"Do you accept? Any thoughts or suggestions?"

I don't have any thoughts or suggestions. I just don't like this job. I wish I could ask whether they have a real culture-related position to offer me. I ask, "Do I have to respond right away?"

"I can tell from the look on your face that you aren't very happy with what I'm offering. Go ahead and think about it and give me a call in the next day or two. Do you want to see the newspaper?"

I say no and thank him. I pick at another piece of my nail, and my finger burns. I squeeze it in my hand, and the pain, like a bright stroke of lightning, burns all the way to the bone. He gives me his number. I grab my purse, no longer a nuisance, and say goodbye. Still sitting, he waves goodbye, saying he'll be waiting for my response. The man who was fumbling with the colored wires has put them all in their places and has immersed himself in the computer on the desk that's up and running. I say a loud goodbye and walk out.

The hallway and the staircase don't look the same way they did when I came up. The walls are closer now and the ceiling lower. As I'm getting into my car, I search for a feeling that can look me straight in the eye and tell me in a loud voice whether this is a good thing or a bad thing. I should make up my mind right now. When I get home, I won't be able to think anymore. The advantages and disadvantages will weave so tightly together that I'll get a headache and abandon any decision. I'm terrified of decisions—they are always wrong. It's a fear I've had since I decided not to come with you. It projects an image of great uncertainty at the end of any road I want to take. But now I have to think. The decision not to be with you was one I made for the rest of my life. Jobs, though, are short-term, here today and gone tomorrow. Choosing them has always been easy. I never cared about the money, how much of my time they took, how they helped advance my career, or whether they were related to my major. A job was either good or bad—I either liked it or I didn't. I didn't even care what you thought. You said, "What are you doing? If you don't want to finish your studies, then don't. But go work with Shabaneh so you can build up your résumé."

I had just come back from Bagh Bookstore alight with joy. I had met an old man named Mr. Ferdowsi, who loved books. I had bought a few books from him and was about to leave when he said they were looking for a bookseller who loves books. Hearing the words "loves books," wings of joy sprouted from my back, and I had felt that was my future embracing me. I was not as well-read as you were. But Mr. Ferdowsi had said that he would teach me everything I needed. We all had only a few courses left. Shabaneh had started an internship at an engineering firm. I wasn't interested in that job. Roja gave private tutoring lessons and wanted to get a master's degree. I didn't want to. And you kept harping on the same string, saying that we should pack up our life and emigrate. Every day you went through and counted an armful of translated documents, recommendation letters, and forms, and put them in an evil, ugly, yellow envelope.

You went to the Mofatteh post office and sent the envelopes out to many corners of the world. East and west and north and south. I hated those envelopes, but I felt assured that you would not leave without me. The only thing I wanted was a job. I wanted it so that I could know where I was going to be the next day and the day after that and in ten years. I wanted to plant you and me like trees in this very land and strengthen our foothold right here so you couldn't go anywhere without me. I didn't want to become an engineer. I was too laissez-faire to be dragged to work early every morning for signatures and contracts. You and Roja used to laugh and say that I was raised like a flower petal wrapped in silk and any hardship would cause me to wither.

That day, though, I had found a job all by myself. In a small bookstore that had customers like you, where you could smell the dust covering the spines coming from the shelves. I had told Mr. Ferdowsi that I didn't care about the pay, that I would start the next day. And I had come home with my joy to share the good news with you. You should have been happy that I had finally realized that even though Dad paid for all my expenses, I needed to work. That we would grow even closer to each other through books. You stood by the kitchen counter, and I paced around the room. I paced and said I wanted to change the way the shelves were arranged and sort the books based on the authors' countries of origin. I said I wanted to tell Mr. Ferdowsi to put an upright piano in a corner so that I could play for the customers. I said that when there were no customers, I would sit in the back and read all the books there so that you would love me more. I said it wasn't fair that you and Roja knew all the books in the world, while I had only read a few insignificant novels. I said once I had read all the books, I would speak to anyone who came to the bookstore, figure out what they liked, and put the best book in their hands. And then I would wait for them to come back one day and tell me that they really liked the book. I said that after a while, we would even open our own bookstore. I said I would keep cleaning my dusty hands on my manteau so much so that when I came back home, it would be dirty down the sides. I showed you my pockets and said, "Look, it would be really dusty here."

And I laughed. But you didn't laugh. You just leaned on the counter, reprimanding me for not realizing that it was not a proper job. You said that I hadn't studied so hard simply to open a bookstore. You said that I should come to my senses before it's too late and that even if I didn't want to continue my studies, I should build up my résumé so I could still get admitted to a foreign school, because you would leave regardless, and we had to be together. You said I had better put my feet firmly on the ground and see real life. You said, "Real life, real like everyone else's, not like your Dad's." I stopped pacing. I lost my wings of joy, and Bagh Bookstore disappeared from my heart. My feet were firmly on the ground, if only you wouldn't take yours off the ground and board that fucking plane. For you, real life was one thing, and my life had nothing to do with that. I wanted to be a teacher, a bookseller, a piano soloist, a journalist. I didn't want to let go of any of my dreams. Whenever I started one, my heart soared toward another; and when I focused on that one, I missed yet another one.

The closer I get to home, the less I want to be there. I wish the traffic jam would never end so I could continue to be stuck between the cars' red and white lights. My heart would be happy with anything but the darkness and silence of the apartment. I want to go out to dinner with some friends. I want us to sit around a semidark restaurant, eat, and laugh out loud at everything in the world. The people at the surrounding tables would frown upon our behavior, and we would keep laughing out loud. I hate arriving home alone like every other day, with nobody there to open the door for me, and having to use my own key. I hate turning on the lights at night, hearing my own voice sometimes, speaking to myself, every time growing more and more afraid that I might be going crazy. I don't want to go home. Not tonight. Roja has a class. Maybe I can go visit Shabaneh. I want to speak with Mahan until morning while he keeps looking at me astounded, merely looking at me and not saying a word, as usual. I stare at my phone and can't make up my mind to dial Shabaneh's number. I am not in the mood for anything. Not the apartment, not Shabaneh, not even myself. I throw my phone in my purse and turn into the darkness of the garage.

As I open the door, the silence of the empty apartment slaps me in the face, and the heavy air collapses on my chest. I open the windows. I turn on the TV to have something alive around me. That movement on the screen will do. It makes me feel like someone is breathing in the apartment, even if they're behind the thick glass screen of the TV. The weak late afternoon light lingers still, but I turn the lights on so that the sadness of the setting sun won't surprise me when it comes. I sit on the red couch and change the channels. There is nothing on to watch. I turn on my laptop. Facebook, my blog, email. Nothing is going on. I should call and ask someone to come over. I should find a job as soon as possible to avoid staying home in the evenings. The empty apartment is driving me crazy. Its walls keep getting closer to one another, and one day not too far away, they will crush me between them. There should be either you or a job. My life can't go on any other way. I have to get a job, no matter what.

TWO

FUCK ME. FUCK ME FOR sitting like a mouse on this chair, staring at the monitor. Fuck me for never learning to express, like a normal human being, what I do and don't want. Fuck me for never having my word be the last word. Today is like every other day, this time is like a thousand other times. I sit at my desk and curse my terrified self. Romeo, my black-sheep plush toy, looks at me from the top of my monitor, saying, "Stupid Shabaneh. You fool." My desk is at the rear of the open-plan office and I like that it is next to the wall. I have a corner of my own and I don't get distracted by people walking past my desk. The space is full of desks and chairs and computers and engineers. They read the misshapen lines on large papers and draw colorful lines on their black screens. Then they get up, drink tea, walk around, ask each other questions, and grab other papers with even more crooked lines from the printer and get busy once again.

There is a quiet buzz in the office. I can't distinguish the words over the slow hum of the air conditioner and the computers' fans and all these engineers breathing next to each other. If a car doesn't drive through the alley outside, sending its noise reverberating inside, I can just close my eyes and pretend I'm sitting at the beach, and that this sound is the sound of the calm sea. Now I just have to take off my shoes and walk on the sand and look at my footprints that remain wet and dark for a few seconds, allowing myself to enjoy the cool breeze coming off the sea and touching my face.

A breeze from the air conditioner passes over Roja's desk and comes straight to my face. There are three desks between hers and mine. Roja sits by the office windows. Like birds, she loves the sky. The moment she arrives, she pulls the blinds all the way up, not caring whether the light reflects off her monitor. When she gets tired, she turns her chair and stares at the persimmon trees in the company's courtyard that, in a month or two, will be full of colors—though she herself will not be here to see their crimson fruits. Roja can't stay put in the closed office and constantly needs to jump up and leave. She hasn't returned yet. My heart breaks whenever I see her empty chair. Arsalan sits by the door on the other side of office. I could never sit in that spot. People walk by his desk on three sides and I don't know how he doesn't get annoyed amid all the hustle and bustle. He's wearing a dark blue T-shirt with pale-blue jeans. From where I sit, I can see his profile, I can see him run his hand through his hair from time to time, turn around to smile at me from where he is sitting at his desk. I am not in the mood for him to get mad at me, so I smile back, a forced, weak smile. He is happy, because he'll get whatever he wants. Today like every other day. This time, too, like a thousand other times.

I had finished my plans, printed them, and was taking them to

Mr. Moghadam. As I walked by the rows of desks, Arsalan followed me with his eyes. When I reached his desk, he called out to me.

"Do you want to go out tonight, talk a bit?"

"Tonight?"

"Yes, after work. I'll drop you off at home after."

"Can we do this some other time? Maybe at the end of the week . . ."

"No, I want to talk."

"Let me take these plans to Mr. Moghadam. He wants to see them."

I didn't look at him and continued on my way. Mr. Moghadam is on the first floor, we're on the third. I walked down the black granite stairs inside the building. I walked slowly to stretch out the time before I would have to answer Arsalan. I checked out the plants on the staircase. The staircase is dark, and the black of the granite makes it seem even darker. The light that came through the dark windows passed through the leaves of the plants that were as tall as me and dappled the floor. One of the leaves of the dieffenbachia plant on the first floor had yellowed, and its sharp point had become dry. I touched the plant's leaves. It was begging me not to let it die. I asked, "What's wrong with you?" I asked, "Do you need some sun? You don't like the black tiles? Do people come light their cigarettes next to you?" I looked at the soil. It didn't have much breath left in it. I moved the soil around with the tip of my fingers. The plant loved it. I should tell Karam Ali to add some mulch to its pot.

The leather-covered door to Mr. Moghadam's office was closed, and his secretary was busy on the phone. She gestured to me to just give her the plans and go. That was good, actually. I was not in the mood to sit with the boss as he went on and on for two hours about the contracts and bids he didn't win, and in the end, he would say,

"Join me tomorrow for the meeting with the Soroush Company." And then I would have to say no, and we would have a fight and he would fire me. Then I would have to sit at home and keep calling this person and that looking for work, and not finding any and having to argue with Mom every day about Mahan. In the end, I would have to take Mahan and leave the house forever and go either to Leyla's or Roja's and no matter how much Dad would call, pleading, trying to talk me into going back, I would not heed him at all.

I walked back up the two floors very slowly, thinking about all this and finally deciding I'd tell Arsalan that I couldn't see him tonight because I was not in the mood. I wouldn't go because I was tired, and I would say I didn't want to discuss it anymore. I won't go, and that's that. But by the time I was standing next to Arsalan's desk, another Shabaneh said, calmly, "Can we just get together another time?"

"No, Shabaneh. I want us to talk. It'll be quick."

"I'm just tired. Besides, I don't want to go out in my work clothes."

"Where do you think we're going? We're not going to a wedding or somewhere you couldn't go in your work clothes. We'll drive to Jamshidiyeh Park, go for a walk, chat, and head back."

I gathered all my strength to ask, "Should I tell the others to join us?"

He jumped up from his seat.

"So the problem isn't that you're tired or your work outfit. You have a problem with me. You don't want to go out with me."

His face turned red. I looked around and was relieved that no one was paying any attention to us. I was afraid that he would raise his voice again.

"Calm down, Arsalan. What are you talking about? I just wondered whether we should . . ."

"You just wondered what? I just said a dozen times that I want to talk to you. You know what, if you don't want to go, we won't go. Just think about it and let me know."

He slammed his pen down on the desk and stared at his monitor. I was afraid he would start another fight in front of everyone. He would stop talking to me again, and whenever I'd look at him, he would frown. I was afraid he would sulk and ruin everything. And then, like in the past, I would be alone, with no one who wants to take me to Jamshidiyeh Park, and I would keep looking at the others going out with their lovers and I would die of the sadness of solitude. So I said, "Okay, let's go."

"You just want to ruin everything, even going out," he murmured while he busied himself with his papers.

He didn't look at me. I waited to see whether or not we were going out in the end. But no matter how long I stood there, he didn't raise his head. I walked back to my own desk. Something would happen, eventually. I passed the other desks and glanced surreptitiously at my colleagues. No one had heard the sound of the pen slamming down on the desk. I sat down and held my head in my hands. My fingers were freezing. I wished I knew whether I should go out with him or not. I listened to the buzzing of the air conditioner, and no matter how hard I tried, I failed to picture myself wearing a colorful pleated skirt and sitting on a beach somewhere by the Mediterranean, waiting for a tall man in a tux and a bow tie to invite me to lunch at a hotel restaurant. I thought to myself, Why am I so terrified of being alone? Why can't I just talk like a normal human being? Why can't I stand by my decisions? Who should I hold responsible? My father? My mother? Or Mahan's illness, after which our life was never the same again? Since when I have become so weak? Maybe since that winter night when the air-raid sirens sounded, and Mom held Mahan close to her breast and screamed, "What can I do with this sick child?"

Mahan had a fever. He would not open his eyes. He was not even crying. He was just breathing fast. Mom had put his little mattress on our red carpet. The power was out, and I hadn't finished my homework. Dad paced around the room, and when he walked past the candle, his terrifying shadow grew larger on the wall. Mom took Mahan's pants off and washed his feet in the little orange plastic tub. Dad brought a plastic bag full of ice. Mom told me to put the ice on Mahan's forehead. I did. His body quivered. Holding on to the bag of ice, I stared at his chest quickly rising and falling. The ice cubes grew smaller and smaller and floated around in the bag full of water. Dad emptied the bag of medications on the table. The air-raid sirens started again. Dad went to the window. The window turned yellow and orange, and then came a horrible sound. The glass in the windows trembled. I dropped the bag of ice and went and stood against the wall. Dad shouted, "Hurry up! Get dressed." My fingers were freezing, and I was sobbing. My tears rolled down into my mouth and tasted like the sea. I had not finished my homework, and Mahan was dying. The sirens started again. Mom took the rest of Mahan's clothes off and poured the water from the tub all over him. His mattress was completely soaked. Dad grabbed him and put him in Mom's arms. Mom said, "Let me take some clothing for them." Then she started crying. Dad picked me up. He said, "There is no need." He threw a blanket over Mahan and pulled Mom's arm.

"Hurry up or the house will collapse on top of us."

I looked at our house, terrified that it would collapse on top of us. I looked at our red carpet. The border made up the streets on which I parked my toy cars; the floral medallions at the center were the park I swung in. I looked at Mahan's mattress and his bed in the corner of the room. At his bag of medications on the table. At the large floor cushions. The crumpled blanket and the ruffled pink pillows embroidered with green-and-red sequined peacocks, souvenirs from Mecca. I looked at our TV cabinet with its wooden door, which we closed when the kids' program ended and decorated with grandma's little quilt. I looked at my notebook and my Persian textbook on the table. At Mom's needlepoint frame, on which I had sewn a white bird in the sky. At the candle flickering on the table and at the terrifying shadows that fell on the wall with every move we made. The house was going to collapse on top of us and that would probably be followed by the needlework falling on the candle, and the table with all the homework I had done would catch fire, and the white needlepoint bird would fly through the bricks and reach my teacher and tell her that night had come and I still hadn't finished my homework. Dad blew out the candle. I closed my eyes and pressed on them hard.

The phone on my desk rings. It's Mr. Moghadam's secretary.

"Can you come down for a second? The corrections on your plans are ready."

I glance at Arsalan, who is busy with his own work. I wish I didn't have to walk past him. But there is no other way. His desk is right by the office door, and the boss is expecting me. I grab my cell phone and start walking, pretending that I'm busy with my phone.

The secretary gives me the plans and smiles at me with her red lipstick. On my way back upstairs, I look at the plans. When did he have the time to make so many corrections? I keep my eyes on the plans and walk past Arsalan's desk. He calls my name. He is kind now, and that means that tonight we are going to Jamshidiyeh.

"I want to order some food. What do you want?"

"Nothing. I'm not hungry."

"Are you upset?"

"No. I just had a big breakfast. And I'm gaining weight. It's better if I don't eat."

"What did Mr. Moghadam say?"

"He made some corrections."

"Do you need help?"

"No, they're not that many. Thanks, though."

I rush back to my desk and sit down. Romeo and one of the other engineers are looking at me. I look down. When I speak to Arsalan, I feel like everyone is watching me and thinking, "What a coward!" Then the ones who know about Mahan will tell those who don't about it, and half an hour later all of them will gather around my desk and talk about me and Mahan and Arsalan. They'll talk until I feel like I'm suffocating and I'll start to cry and gather my things and leave the company forever.

I unroll the plans. I am hungry and not at all in the mood for work. I wish today would end and I could go home. Mahan is at home. Mom has probably cooked something. My phone rings. It's Roja. I look at her empty desk and check the clock. She should have been here by now. She says her appointment went longer than she expected and she is now having lunch with Leyla. She says she'll come when she's done with lunch. I so wish I were there with them. I want restaurant food and my own friends. Friends who care for me.

"What are you having?"

"Pizza and lasagna. I'll bring you some lasagna."

The monster in my belly begins to roar. I look around and pray that no one has heard it. Goli is laughing. I miss Leyla. I miss sitting next to her and chatting. Leyla understands me more than anyone. Like Misagh. I tell Roja to pass Leyla the phone. I want to tell her that I have to go out with Arsalan tonight and ask her what I should do now. But I change my mind and don't tell her anything. She would probably feel uncomfortable talking about it at lunch. She would probably not be in the mood to listen to my constant talk about Arsalan. I ask how she is doing and tell her I'll explain everything later. I'm starving. Leyla asks, "Do you want anything?"

"A sandwich."

"I'll tell Roja to get you one. What kind?"

I look at Arsalan, who looks annoyed as he works. I'd get in trouble if I eat without him. He would say I didn't want to eat with him, and why didn't I, and then he wouldn't listen to me explain. He would shout and then leave. I tell Leyla, "You know what, I don't want anything. Don't worry about it. We'll go grab something together some other time."

"Are you sure?"

I have to talk to Leyla. "Yes. I'll call you tonight. I need to talk to you."

"I'll be waiting for your call."

Arsalan had also said, "I'll be waiting for you," and gone downstairs. Misagh had just left the country. It was dark, and the first snow of the year had just started. In the light of the streetlight, I could see tiny snowflakes overtaking each other and rushing down. The ground was soaked. No one was at work, and Karam Ali was collecting the mugs and glasses from the desks. I wrapped the white wool scarf that I had knitted myself around my neck and pulled it up all the way to my nose. I didn't want to go downstairs. I wished I had a phoenix feather I could set on fire to have the bird appear like Nils from *The Wonderful Adventures of Nils,* pick me up, and place me in the morning of the following day. I took my time putting on my coat, doing all the buttons, each one slower than the previous one. I swung my backpack onto my back, dug my hands in my pockets, and said goodbye to Karam Ali the longest way I knew how, and then left the building. Arsalan was waiting for me in his dusty-green Saipa Pride. He rolled the window down and, unlike other times, he didn't smile at me. He said, "Get in the car."

It was my first time getting into his car. The shoulders of my coat were already wet. The snow fell fast and kept covering the windshield. I had to say something to stop him from saying what I did not want to hear. "The snowflakes are tiny. They'll cover everything. My brother loves playing in the snow. He's probably sitting by the window right now and looking out at the street."

He didn't say anything. His silence blended with the scraping sound of the wipers pushing the snow to the lower corners of the windshield. Traffic was heavy, and the red rear lights of the car in front reflected on Arsalan's face. With my finger, I drew a circle in the fog on my window, adding eyes and a nose and a mouth. The silence was driving me crazy. I was growing really upset. He probably sensed it. "Where should we go?" he asked.

"I don't know. I should go home soon to help my brother with his homework."

"Okay, so I'll get right to the point."

I searched his face for the fun, smiling Arsalan I had seen at work for the past six months. The guy who, on his first day on the job, had bought ice cream for everyone and then, in a loud voice, asked everyone he didn't know how they were doing. By the end of that day he had made several good friends. The guy for whom work was like going to university. He had graduated top of his class from Amirkabir University with a lot of work experience and had signed on to the job with a high-paying contract. The guy who called a different restaurant every day to order food and used every opportunity to have fun and tease everyone, even Roja. That night, I could not find traces of the guy he usually was. He was cold and serious. He began driving in the direction of my home and started talking.

He said he had lost his father and lived with his mother and loved her so much. He said his mother had been a teacher and now she was retired, and that they lived in a small apartment on Malek Street. He didn't say how his father had died, and I immediately began imagining a dozen reasons for his death, each more beautiful and sadder than the last. He said he had fallen for me because I was simple and minded my own business. He said he had noticed how, that one time at work when Mr. Moghadam had complained for no good reason and shouted at me, instead of arguing, I had looked at him with a smile and listened to what he was saying. He said he had noticed how I never laughed out loud, did not shout, was never in a bad mood. He said my smile was peaceful, that he was only looking for peace in a relationship, nothing else. And that his father's death had reminded him how short life is and that it wasn't worth wasting the remaining years of his life worrying. He finished by saying that if we were together, he would make sure I had everything I needed. I drew wavy hair around the face I had traced on the window. I drew two bows on the two sides of her head, a shirt, and a skirt. The figure, with her puffed sleeves and ruffled skirt, had become my nanny, raising me since childhood instead of my queen mother, and now she had arrived to answer Arsalan for me. For a noblewoman like me it would be inappropriate to respond directly myself. Arsalan didn't ask me anything about me. Not about my likes and dislikes, my parents, my home, anything. That was best. I don't like talking to people about Mahan. I erased the nanny with the back of my hand. It grew very cold. We had reached my address. Arsalan didn't smile. In a cold, serious tone, he told me to think about what he had said, because he wanted to know where he stood with me from now on. I was annoyed. I didn't want to hear any of this. I was more comfortable with his flirtatious greetings and teasing. That way there were no expectations, no responsibilities. I didn't want to think about whether I loved him or not. But now he had forced me to. When I got out of the car, he reached out and held the door, not letting me close it. Once again he said that he would wait for my response, then closed the car door and left.

Roja comes in and calls out with a big hello. Her hands are, as always, full. She has cut her red hair short and has bangs. She puts a red folder on her desk, throws her purse on the folder, and puts her glasses to the side. She still has a big bag in her hand. With tired, slow steps she walks toward me, pats Romeo on the head, and leaves the bag on my desk.

"You haven't had lunch yet, right?"

I glance toward Arsalan. He is watching us. Roja follows my eyes and turns around and waves at Arsalan. Arsalan rises halfway in his chair. Roja looks at me.

"What's going on? He seems to be in a mood."

"No, he's fine. Did Leyla go to the newspaper?"

"She did, but she wasn't feeling well. She was talking about Misagh again today. Unwrap this and eat. It's lasagna."

"Misagh?"

"Yes, she was thinking about him."

"She's always thinking about him."

Misagh. Kind Misagh. How much I miss him. If he were here, I could talk to him as much as I wanted. I could ask him whether I should go out with Arsalan today or not, what I should do about him in general. Or perhaps I could ask him to go and talk to Arsalan himself, and then I would do whatever he told me to do and not have to worry about anything. Roja opens the plastic bag and takes the lid off the container. The smell of cheese and sauce wafts up from my desk. Roja takes a plastic fork out of the bag and sticks it in the lasagna.

"Eat, before it gets cold. Why isn't anyone eating properly today?"

She goes back to her desk, turns the computer on, swivels her chair around, and stares out the window. I eat a bite of the lasagna, and my eyes fall on Arsalan, who is busy working. I wish Mahan was here. It's been so long since I took him to a restaurant. I put the lid back on the container and unroll the plans again. Mr. Moghadam has decreased the length of the shafts, which decreases the reliability factor. Perhaps the costs were too high. I am not in the mood to correct them. I just want to go home now, lie down on my bed, and read a romance novel. I've told myself a hundred times I should bring a book to work with me and leave it in my desk drawer for moments like these, and I always forget. I collect the plans, pick up Romeo, and open the folder marked "literature" on my desktop to start looking for a good ebook. I open Bukowski's unpublished stories. I read the first paragraph and don't understand what I'm reading. I read it again—nothing. Both times, when I reach the middle of the second sentence, my mind wanders to strange places. I wish I had a real work of classic literature, something like *The Red and the Black.* One of those heavy books that tires your arms just to hold them up, but you still can't stop reading. I would read it and live vicariously through Madame de Rênal. I would sit with my long, lined skirt in front of the fireplace and busy myself doing broderie; I would think of Julien and cry because I could not see him. I should look up the meaning of the word *broderie.* I've read it for the past twenty years and I still don't know what it is exactly. I look at the clock. It's just three thirty, and I have to stay here for a thousand more hours until I have to go out with Arsalan and walk by his side and pretend to be in love and happy.

I have to pretend to be happy. It's the only thing I know how to do well. All of us have always done that—pretend. Me, Mom, Dad. Among us it is just Mahan who always seems to be actually happy. Who knows. He doesn't really talk properly, so maybe he too is pretending like the rest of us. Like that time when Mom's miserable life got to the point that Dad took us all on a family vacation so that we would feel happy, and Mahan threw up the whole way and made a mess all over the car. Or that time when we went to Mahan's school and listened to the song he performed with his classmates and none of us understood a thing, but we listened and applauded them nonetheless with fake smiles. Or the day I was admitted to university and Mom threw a party and left Mahan at Grandma's so that he wouldn't embarrass us in front of people. We have been pretending for a long time, conjuring up a simple happiness that we've lost to this indefinite eternal misery. When did it start? Where? What day? I remember it took us several months to realize we had to forget about happiness forever. Something had been added to our lives. Something like a huge dark monster who always walked alongside Mahan, throwing its ugly shadow over him. I could see it with its ugly, filthy teeth, standing between Mom and Mahan and laughing.

Mom had Mahan standing in front of her, for the thousandth time. She told me to take two steps back. I was afraid, but I didn't make a sound, because Mom had told me not to. Mom held Mahan under his arms.

"Stand up, little one. Now walk to your sister."

Then she let him go and gave him a little push toward me. Mahan's knees buckled, and he fell. Mom was sweating, and locks of her black hair were plastered on her neck and forehead. She held him up again. She was panting.

"Get up, my little boy. Look at your sister. It's just two steps. Go on."

She had Mahan stand up again and let him go. Mahan fell on his face. I cried. I begged her.

"Leave him alone, Mom. He doesn't deserve this."

"Didn't I tell you not to say anything? Don't move. When he walks toward you, catch him in your arms."

I kept standing there. Mahan would fall, but he would not cry. Every time he fell, he would just raise his head up from the floor and look at me with imploring eyes. I kept sobbing and imagined that Mahan would die by the time Dad got home, and then we would have to wrap him in a white sheet like Grandpa and leave him among the rocks in the soil and keep crying. I imagined that Mom would put Mahan's toys and cars by the door, like Grandpa's walking stick and clothes, so that the salt peddler would take them all and give us salt rocks in exchange. And I thought about how lonely I would feel without him. I was sobbing for dead Mahan, and Mom would not stop. She kept having him stand, and Mahan wasn't even touching the floor with his feet. He was gliding out of Mom's hand and spreading on the floor. The sound of a suffocating bird left Mahan's throat, and he fell once again. Mom screamed and slapped him.

"Stand up! I'm telling you to stand up!"

I ran and hugged Mahan.

"For God's sake, leave him alone, Mom. You're killing him."

Mom leaned on the wall and knocked her head against it. *Tap. Tap. Tap.* The sound of her head banging on the wall swirled around in my head. She shouted, "I wish he had died."

I held Mahan, heavy in my arms, and carried him to the end of the living room. I leaned against the wall and sat him on my legs. He looked at the apartment as if he were seeing it for the first time. A smile played at the corners of his lips. I threw my arms around him and sobbed. I loved him. I didn't want him to die. I kept crying and Mahan kept smiling until we heard Dad's keys in the lock. Dad opened the door and came in. He had a box of sweets in one hand and two big gift-wrapped boxes. Mahan opened his arms for Dad. I murmured a hello, but my greeting got lost in my sobs. Dad looked at us and asked, "What now?"

"You hide in that goddamn office of yours from dawn to dusk and haven't noticed that this child can't walk yet," she shouted.

Dad put the box of sweets and the gifts on the table. Mahan crawled toward them. Dad held his hand toward me. I got up. "So what? He's not walking. Don't you know that he's sick?" he retorted.

"He is not sick. He is dumb."

"No, he is sick. You need to leave him alone. Go take your medication. I bought us a cake."

Mom snapped at him, "Who told you to get a cake?"

"I told myself. You invite more than thirty people over for Shabaneh's birthday, but for this kid's you don't even invite your own mother."

"Invite them over so they can see that my son is two years old and all he can do is stare?"

Mahan held on to the legs of the table and tried to stand up. I was afraid that he would fall. I grabbed the gifts and put them on the floor. Mahan sat back down. He banged on the boxes and laughed. Dad turned to me.

"Get up, my love. Get some matchsticks so we can light the candles."

"Get up, Shabaneh. Let's go have some tea," Roja says.

I put Romeo back on the monitor and follow Roja to the break room. It's dark in there. Roja picks up the teapot. I put the mugs in front of her for her to pour us tea. The tea in the pot is overbrewed and too dark. "Do you have tea bags?" she asks.

"No."

She goes out and comes back with two bags of Nescafé.

"I got them from Goli."

I pour us some hot water and sit at the table. For the thousandth time I stare at the little yellow flowers of the plastic tablecloth. Roja empties the coffee bags into the water and stirs them. "I'll deposit another two million today for Arsalan. I'll still owe him five million and I'm not sure when I can give it back," she says.

"Don't worry. He doesn't need it now."

Roja holds the mug in front of her mouth and blows to cool it down. Her glasses fog up.

"Will you let me know if he needs it? He might just be too polite and not tell me."

Before I can ask Roja what I should do about the evening, Goli comes in. She pours herself some tea and joins our conversation.

"How are you, Shabaneh? Why do you always sit there all day long, brooding like a Qajari woman at a gathering? Just as Arsalan makes such a racket, you sit there quietly. If you keep being so shy, you'll get screwed. What's there to think about? And you don't eat until your BFF arrives. I mean Roja, of course, not the other one!"

I smile. This is the thousandth time I've forced myself to smile today.

"Where's your other BFF? He doesn't mind you drinking tea all by yourself?"

Now I am annoyed and upset. I hate people who look me in the eye and presume to discuss my life. If it weren't for people like her, I wouldn't be tied to Arsalan right now. Roja says it's my own fault that I go everywhere with Arsalan in front of everyone. Okay, I do, but I don't joke with them about their lives. It's so good that Roja is here and I don't have to be alone with Goli. Roja always knows how to react without getting embarrassed about anything. She turns toward me and says, "Goli is jealous because she doesn't have a boyfriend herself."

Goli cracks up and sits down. She keeps talking and talking. I look at the tablecloth and squint. I connect the flowers to one another and create squares, circles, and hearts out of them. No matter how hard I try, they don't turn into triangles. I turn into a little kid and start playing hopscotch between the small squares and large circles full of flowers, and the yellow of the chamomiles smears my pink skirt and white apron. When I get home in the evening, the nanny reprimands me, but when I tell her that I've seen her steal some sweets for her child and threaten to tell my queen mom, she's nice again, and we decide that we won't say anything to anyone. I listen to Goli's voice. It sounds like the dubbed voices of foreign cartoons. Perhaps my tutor, kind and beautiful like Jane Eyre, speaks like that. If Goli stopped talking so much nonsense, I could listen to her voice for hours and hours. I love the way she pronounces her *s*. I try to imitate her pronunciation with my tongue. Someone calls me from the office.

"Shabaneh, phone call for you."

I pick my half-finished Nescafé and get up.

I thank Goli, then turn to Roja and say, "I'll find you later to chat."

"Sorry I interrupted you. Were you having a private conversation?" Goli asks.

I leave Roja to answer her. Mr. Moghadam's secretary is on the line.

"Darling, tomorrow you have a meeting at Soroush Company."

Tomorrow? Tomorrow is Monday and Mahan has an art class at six.

"I can't tomorrow."

"Mr. Moghadam told me to tell you that you have to be there. Apparently they are closing the deal. Do you want me to put you through so you can discuss it with him directly?"

It'll be of no use to talk to Mr. Moghadam. I have to go.

"No, I'll figure something out."

"Thanks, love."

I hang up and think about who can take Mahan to class tomorrow. Dad is at work, and Mom won't take him. As always, she thinks it's useless.

"You are torturing him for no reason. Do you really think this kid is going to turn into an artist?"

"Mom, he isn't a kid. He's twice as tall as I am. And he loves painting."

"I'm talking about the fact that he has the mind of a four-year-old. His classmates make fun of him. Why don't you understand such simple things?"

"That's enough, Mom. Nobody makes fun of him. I'll take him to class, and you'll see how good he is."

I wanted to ask her, "When is this resentment of yours toward Mahan going to come to an end? When will you realize your misery isn't all because of him? When will you learn to love him?" But I didn't say any of this. I swallowed my words and slammed the door behind me with the pressure of all the unsaid words stuck in my throat. Mahan had already left the house and was waiting for me in the cab. I had him wear his new pair of jeans with his brown velvet coat and combed his hair to the side. I looked at him from a distance, sitting in the back seat of the cab, leaning his forehead on the window. My heart felt weak for him. He had become a handsome young man.

Leyla had given me the information about the class. She had heard about it from the graphic designer at the magazine where she worked. The class wasn't for people with special needs. It was for children under ten, and I wasn't sure whether they would accept Mahan, who was twenty-two. Mahan was so excited for the class that he didn't ask for anything on the way there. He just asked, four or five times, "Is it going to be a good class?" And I replied, "Yes, very good. Leyla recommended it." When he heard Leyla's name he calmed down, but only for a few minutes, until he asked once again, "Is it going to be a good class?" The driver, like all other drivers, kept glancing at us in the rearview mirror. I had learned not to get angry because of all the eyes staring at Mahan. When we arrived, I played an audiobook of *The Little Prince* for Mahan on an MP3 player and asked him to wait in the car and be a good boy until I got back. The other kids had not yet arrived, and the instructor was arranging the paint cans on the table. I called out to him and told him that Mister So-and-so at the so-and-so magazine had told me about him and praised his work with kids. Then I told him, "My brother is 'mentally challenged,' but I think he has a talent for art."

The instructor gave me a surprised look. Once again my misery started up. Why shouldn't people know the meaning of these two English words, forcing me to explain that I meant he suffered from a disability? How I hated those words and how I wanted to escape them, but nobody seemed to realize that. He said that the class was for "normal kids," and parents of other kids might oppose Mahan's presence in class. He said my brother had to be trained in a specialized school for people like him. As if I didn't know all that already. It was as if I weren't the one who had lived with him for twenty-two years and knew better than anyone what school was suitable for him and which one was not. I had readied myself to insist, to beg, to tell him my brother was kind and quiet and wouldn't harm anyone. I wanted to pull out Mahan's drawings and throw his talents in the instructor's face and in the face of any person who said Mahan was not normal. But I couldn't do any of that. Like a good, well-mannered girl, I just took his drawings out of the folder and showed them to the instructor.

"A few months ago, a friend of mine gave him some paint for his birthday, and since then he has done nothing but paint and he's already finished several jars of color. Even if you can't accept him, can you just take a look at these and let me know if he has any talent?"

The instructor studied the drawings closely.

"Is your brother with you?"

Through the window, I pointed out Mahan, who was sitting there calmly in the cab, leaning his head on the window and listening on his headphones.

"To tell you the truth, I've never worked with special-needs kids, but if you can accompany him and sit through the class with him, I don't mind trying it out. Can you wait for this class to end?"

We waited. We went and had ice cream. We went to a bookstore and bought more paint and pastels and a bag of thirty-six markers. The instructor accepted him. Mahan loves his art class. He waits all week for Monday to come. I have to find someone to take him to class. Leyla is a good option. Mahan loves her even more than Mom. I write on the sticky note on my desk: "Call Leyla for Mahan's class."

"Everyone, listen up for a second!"

It's Mr. Kazemi, the company's financial manager. The humdrum of the open plan quiets down for a moment, and my ears can take a break. "Everyone has to bring the necessary documents for insurance applications tomorrow. Three photos, a copy of front and back of your national ID card, and all the pages of your birth certificate. Those who were previously insured also need to bring their previous insurance number. Please pick up the forms by the door before leaving today," he announced.

Roja suddenly appears at my desk, tickled pink.

"I probably don't need to bring my documents. What do you think? I'll probably be gone in a few weeks."

She utters "gone" with such joy that I can't tell her she should submit her documents regardless, that maybe something will happen and she won't leave. I hide my sadness over her leaving and say, "You're right. No need to bring them. Why bother."

I think about my own documents. My birth certificate and ID card, and their copies, are all ready in the black bag under the bed. When Dad hears that I'm getting insurance, he'll burst with joy. His only issue with my job was that they didn't provide insurance. Otherwise, just as he'd hoped, his daughter had gone to university and become an engineer—making up for his sick son. The only thing left was that she was uninsured. He kept looking for a government job that would offer insurance, kept telling me how being insured was important for my future and for my retirement. He would end his lecture with, "Think about your future and leave the company. In ten years, in twenty years, in thirty years . . ." So far, six of those years have passed, and I've turned twenty-eight without being insured at work. Dad doesn't know that I don't dare change the way things are. I wouldn't dare leave my position at this company, even if they didn't pay me. Dad doesn't know I've even been using my worn-out wallet for the past three years, never even taking it out in front of anyone. Every time I've decided to swap it out for the new wallet Arsalan bought me, my heart has swelled and all my memories with the old wallet have rushed before my eyes, and I eventually fail to replace it. Dad doesn't know these things. He only knows that I go to work, and he imagines that I'm happy. He thinks his daughter is a strong and successful engineer who can move mountains, an engineer whose future he does not need to worry about. Dad does not know a lot of things.

I open my wallet and take out the little envelope of passport photographs I keep inside. There is only one photo left. I should go take a new one. The photo lab is right around the corner. I take my mirror out of my backpack and pass a hand over my eyebrows. They need threading. My face looks uglier and duller than ever, and two dark circles, exactly like Mom's, have formed under my eyes. I squint and stare at the two wrinkles that start at the corner of my eyes, one going up, the other going down. I'll just have the photo I already have reprinted, again.

The guys are gathering around Arsalan's desk. They tease one another and for some unknowable reason they all burst out laughing, and their laughter fills the office. Goli bangs on her desk.

"Guys, please!"

They turn silent for a moment before raising their voices again. It's like they're on campus. Hamed is there too, and he laughs out loud exactly like Arsalan. Hamed, our good old college friend, who didn't like Arsalan. It had only been a month since Arsalan had been hired at the company. Hamed had a fight with Mr. Moghadam. He had handed his resignation to the secretary, collected his stuff, and was on his way out. I had taken the letter back from the secretary and asked her to not say anything to Mr. Moghadam. I had talked Hamed into staying, and we were talking by the plants on the staircase. I was asking him to not take things so hard, that the conditions would be more or less the same wherever he went, when Arsalan, with his usual grin that caused his left eyebrow and the left corner of his lips to turn upward, walked down the stairs and, reaching Hamed, tapped him on the chest.

"Keep your distance, Hamed. This lady is taken."

Then he winked at both of us and left. I froze. Hamed asked me in surprise, "Are you two together?"

"No, I have no clue why he just said that."

I didn't know Arsalan well, but he looked at me in a way that I liked. Some days he passed by my desk and joked about some other colleague and we laughed. Then he would move things around on my desk and in the end would pick up Romeo from the top of my computer, throw him in my face, and walk away. The first time I was shocked, but after that I learned to grab Romeo and laugh along with Arsalan. I don't know why, but I didn't want Hamed to dislike Arsalan. "He just jokes around a lot," I explained.

"That's not a funny joke. Be careful with him!"

The guys' laughter gets loud again. It's five thirty. Goli picks up her stuff, says something under her breath, and leaves the office, irritated. Arsalan isn't afraid of anyone. Not Goli, not Mr. Moghadam, nor anyone else. He's the boss of all the guys. He's everyone's boss.

They say girls like strong guys, guys who support them, big handsome guys, guys who don't mess around and don't cheat, quiet guys, guys they can mother, guys who are happy and joke around, guys who are constantly kind to them, guys who . . . but I don't love Arsalan. The more I look at him, the more I realize that I don't love him. I don't know why. I don't dislike the way he looks. His light-colored eyes that look like marbles, and his curly black hair that looks like Romeo's and that Roja says looks tacky. The smooth pale skin of his face, which is always covered in a sparse stubble. His being tall and his simple style. His unstoppable laughter and his great appetite for life, like Roja. I don't even dislike his being skinny. But there is something about him that rubs me the wrong way, and I don't even know what it is. I don't know why he likes me. I'm fat, I'm not eloquent, I don't know how to joke around, I've never made anyone laugh, and my clothes are always simple and dark. I can't even wear mascara for fear that the tears that come out of nowhere will draw two parallel black lines from my eyes to my chin. I don't know what he loves in me, and that is what terrifies me. This vast, shapeless unknowing that throws me into a dark, unfamiliar place. I'm afraid that, one day, the place we're in will turn dark, and Arsalan's eyes will turn red and twinkle and he'll show me his hooves and, laughing, he'll insert his long canine teeth into my neck. Something is happening between the two of us, and I don't know why it is happening, and that frightens me.

I always thought that he should like Roja, not me. Roja suits Arsalan more than me. She is beautiful and tall, bronzes her skin, and wears red lipstick without any shame, and her eyebrows are always in shape. Roja never cries, and her eyes are always made-up. She goes go-karting and wins against all the guys. I don't even know how to drive, and no matter what they say, I don't believe a go-kart is the same as a normal car. I didn't believe it that day either. Friday morning, eight in the morning. Arsalan had arranged for everyone at work to meet at the go-karts. He said we would eat breakfast there and then start. No one could figure out how he had talked Mr. Moghadam not only into coming but also into offering a gold coin as a prize for first place. I thought about the high speed and the winding corners and the open go-kart, and something dropped in my heart. I was worried that when I got there, I'd be forced to get into a go-kart and speed away, that I wouldn't find the brake and the kart would turn over and my foot would be trapped among the metal scraps and need to be cut off and then Mom wouldn't even have one healthy child. Then she would go insane and I would have to spend the rest of my life limping with a cane to and from the asylum. I said I wasn't going. Roja got mad at me.

"You act like an old woman."

She called Leyla and urged her to go with her. She said speed and excitement were good for her spirits. When they got back, she showed me her gold coin and said, "Didn't I tell you I'd win first prize? Arsalan was looking for you. When he realized you weren't there, he was very disappointed."

Then her eyes looked mischievous, and she added, "He's not a bad guy; I just don't know why he wants to play boss all the time. One of these days I'll have to put him in his place."

And Leyla laughed for the first time in ages.

Hamed says goodbye. Roja says, "Wait. Give me a ride. I don't have my car."

She stands up and gets her stuff. She bundles everything in her arms, and her red folder drops to the floor. I get up, gather her documents, and hand them to her. I should ask her to talk to Arsalan again. They understand each other. The last time they talked, everything got better. "Are you heading out?" I ask.

"Yes, I'm tutoring. Why haven't you left yet?"

The top of her green scarf is wrinkled. I smooth it out. It matches her eyes perfectly; no one else has eyes like hers.

"Arsalan asked me to go out with him tonight."

"Isn't that a good thing? Why do you look like you're in mourning? Just go and have fun."

I look down and say in a low whisper, "It's not fun when it's just the two of us."

She gives me the same advice she has given me dozens of times.

"Arsalan is right to want to go out with you and have fun, Shabaneh. If you don't enjoy being with him, you should end it."

She pulls her purse onto her shoulder.

"If you don't like Arsalan, you should tell him. You act so weird around him that if I were in his shoes, I'd also think you were in love with me."

I murmur, "Yes, you're right," in such a low voice that even I have a hard time hearing myself.

"Do you really not love him?"

She asks the question in such a way that there is no need for me to respond. Her eyes full of mischief, she laughs and rushes out.

The office is almost empty now, and its calming humdrum is gone. Karam Ali comes upstairs and begins clearing the desks of mugs and glasses. My stomach turns. Arsalan isn't at his desk, so I can't ask him when we're leaving or if we're going out at all. What if we don't go, and he realizes that I don't love him? What if we do go and have a fight right there and then, and he screams at me in front of everyone and I push him down the mountain and get a life sentence and Mahan has to remain all alone? I sit at my desk and imagine Mahan having to come visit me in prison. I should tell Mom not to bring him with her. It would be hard for him to see me through the glass of the visiting hall.

"Call Leyla for Mahan's class."

I pick up the phone and dial Leyla's number.

"The person you are trying to reach is currently unavailable."

"Well, shall we go, Shabaneh?"

I feel like someone just poured a glass of ice water down my back. Arsalan dries his hands in a handkerchief and studies the take-out bag.

"What is this?"

"Lasagna. Roja brought it."

He shrugs. He is not happy with me. He stops himself from asking why I didn't have lunch with him, why I acted so stubborn and said I was not hungry. I have the stupid idea of saying, "It's for Mahan."

Then I get mad at myself for lying for the sake of not making him upset.

"Who were you calling?"

"Leyla."

I get up, collect my things, and put them in my backpack. His face is full of questions. I want to annoy him by not explaining why I was calling her. I want to be stubborn, to be strong and mischievous, but instead, like a good girl, I explain, "I have to take Mahan to his art class tomorrow evening, but Mr. Moghadam needs me to go to Soroush Company. I was hoping Leyla could take him."

"Why didn't you ask me? I'll take him."

I stare at his face. I try to understand whether he's just saying this to be polite or if he really means it, and if he does mean it, whether he wants to do it because he's curious about spending time with someone with special needs or whether he really loves Mahan. I can't tell anything from his features. I'm afraid he might annoy Mahan, ask him too many questions and make fun of him, or take him to his friends so *they* can all gather around him and laugh at him, or not hold Mahan's hand on the street and a car might hit him and Arsalan would be rid of him forever.

"Thanks, but there's no need. I think Leyla can take him."

"Why not? Mahan gets along well with me. You said so yourself.

That time we went out, he sat next to me the whole time. Don't you remember?"

I remember. He had invited me, Leyla, Roja, and two or three of his friends to Farahzad Gardens, to celebrate the beginning of our relationship. He had insisted that I bring my brother too. He knew about Mahan's condition, so the invitation made me angry.

"My brother is not a puppet for your entertainment."

"My dear, who said I wanted to make fun of him?"

"So why are you insisting that I bring him?"

"Because he's your brother. Because you love him. And I want to meet him."

"My brother has a hard time with strangers."

"I won't invite any strangers. We'll invite whoever you want, whoever Mahan is comfortable with."

Arsalan didn't bring his friends, and I took Mahan. Mahan liked Arsalan. I could see it in his eyes. I could tell from the way he sat like a gentleman next to Arsalan on the wooden bench, holding his head high and not shying away from Arsalan's questions. Arsalan had bought him a blue watch and a beret, like the one Misagh used to wear in college. And I almost wished Arsalan would wear one of those hats and look like Misagh. When Mahan wanted to go to the restroom, Arsalan got up too. "The men will go together!"

Leyla squeezed my knee, not letting me go after them. "He's right. Let the men go together!" she said. I followed them with my eyes from a distance as they walked hand in hand, and when they got back, Mahan's sleeve was wet, and he looked frightened but he was laughing. But now I'm afraid he might go so far with Arsalan that I can't follow him with my eyes. I'm afraid he won't listen to what Arsalan says or will do things that could make others think less of him. Mahan is the best brother in the world, but nobody other than me gets that. I cannot let him go to class with Arsalan.

"I should ask him and see what he prefers."

"Ask Mahan?"

"Of course. I should ask him who he'd rather go to class with."

He looks at me with such surprise—as if Mahan doesn't know how to think and can't know what he likes or doesn't like. I'm irritated by Arsalan's ignorance. I grab my backpack and walk out with him. I hold my head low and go down the stairs ahead of him, as fast as I can, hoping that no one will see us.

The sun has set, and it's not that hot anymore. I sit in the car. Arsalan buckles his seat belt.

"Jamshidiyeh Park?"

Why does he even ask me when he has already made up his mind? I roll the window down. He turns onto Valiasr Street but doesn't speed up enough for the wind to blow into my face and bring tears to my eyes and dry out my lips. I look at him changing the gears, lost in thought. I wish I loved him. Then I would ask him out of nowhere to stop the car, and I would hug him tight and tell him all the romantic words I've kept to myself all these years for no good reason. I would even grab his hand the moment we sat in the car and wouldn't let it go and would have him change the gear with his left hand. We would become like Leyla and Misagh. Like when I counted the hours until I could go out with them and sit in the middle of the back seat and stare at their fingers locked together on the stick shift. When we arrived at the park and walked side by side, I would get close to him and touch his arm with my arm, and dozens of little birds would begin to jump up and down in my heart. Like Leyla, who would stare at Misagh when he talked and lean her head on his shoulder and laugh, and the little birds in her heart would appear in her eyes. I would run in front of them and walk backward to see Leyla playing with the ring Misagh had just bought her and that was too big for her, thinking nobody would see her. If I loved Arsalan, I would always wear a long, ruffled skirt and I would know what to do so everybody would look at us and think to themselves, How happy those two are.

I look at Arsalan's fingers holding listlessly onto the steering wheel. I look at my own fingers that look like those of a student, nervous before an exam, perched on my knees, orderly but anxious. I could reach out and hold his hand right now. I hold my breath. I raise my hand from my knee. Arsalan suddenly punches the horn in the middle of the steering wheel and keeps his hand there for a few seconds, and the curse he whispers under his breath gets lost in the sound of the horn.

"Who drops off a passenger in the middle of the road?"

"Where else should he drop them off when the traffic light is right here? The guy is just trying to make a living."

He gestures toward me in a way that shouts, "Nonsense"—I can hear him in my head. He looks the other way and once again sounds the horn. He sounds it to show me he isn't listening to me and it doesn't matter at all what nonsense I'm saying. I withdraw and move to the right edge of the seat. His shouting rattles in my head like Mrs. Pepperpot's spoon. I feel like I'm growing smaller and smaller, and my feet begin to move farther and farther away from the car floor. Whenever he gets angry I turn into the very little Shabaneh my mom scolded.

Yasaman's mom slammed the door. Mom turned toward me and the sound of her slapping me in the face caused the world to pause for a moment.

"The last thing we needed was this stupid kid becoming a thief too! What were you doing there?"

We had been playing in the yard with Yasaman. We had thrown her glass marbles in my cooking pot. We had picked apart several flowers and thrown them over the marbles and kept stirring them together to make a stew of marbles and flowers. Mahan had annoyed Mom, so I had brought him outside with me. Mom had a headache and she couldn't tolerate her stupid child. I was playing Mahan's mom and Yasaman his aunt. He moved around us and brought us flowers. We had run out of rice and sugar cubes. I asked Mahan to watch over the stew and not let it burn, and Yasaman and I went pretend grocery shopping. When we got back, the marbles were not there. I asked Mahan a hundred times, "Did you take the marbles?" but he didn't respond. His eyes looked empty. I held his shoulders and shook him.

"Mahan, give the marbles back. For God's sake, give them back."

He didn't. He didn't move at all. Yasaman got mad at me and walked back to her apartment. Mahan and I opened the door to ours quietly and went to our room. We sat there in silence so as not to wake Mom up. They rang the bell. Mom got up. She had a kerchief around her head. Her hair was disheveled, and she had two dark circles around her eyes. Yasaman's mother was at the door. She said if we couldn't take care of Mahan so that he didn't bother other kids, we had better have him admitted. Mom shut the door on her.

I'm twenty-eight now, but whenever someone shouts at me I still withdraw and become little so that I can hide within myself. We are stuck in the traffic on Valiasr Street and I'm a tiny Mrs. Pepperpot with a heavy spoon around my neck.

"I'm sorry. I shouldn't have gotten angry."

I don't know what he saw in my face to make him suddenly

become kind. When he apologizes, my muscles relax, and something begins to bubble up in my heart and bring tears to my eyes. The red lights of the cars in front of us turn into blurry hexagons. I stare up at the roof of the car to stop the tears from rolling down my cheeks.

"I'm trying to control my temper more, Shabaneh, but it's impossible. I swear to God, if you were driving, you would know how awful and nerve-racking driving is in this city."

He has released the slingshot elastic and a large stone has just hit me. How mean of him! Does he have to constantly remind me that I don't know how to drive? I swallow the hard lump in my throat and say in a low voice, "I'll learn one of these days."

"I'll teach you myself. What good am I for if I don't?"

He puts his hand on my knee and smiles. He soon takes it back because he has to turn onto Jamaran Street. I turn on the car stereo. A rap song with a fast beat comes on. I turn the volume up and I'm still trying to figure out what language they're rapping in when he turns it off.

"You don't like this kind of music. Let's talk."

"About what?"

"About everything. Life. Whatever you like."

What do I like to talk about? I would like to talk about all the things that cling to my brain and pull it in all directions. I would like to ask him to be like Misagh. Please be like Misagh. Exactly like him. Patient and calm. I shouldn't be constantly worried when I'm with you. Learn to look at me the way Misagh looked at Leyla, letting me show you whatever worries I have in my heart. I would like to speak about Mahan, who is a piece of me that doesn't live inside me. I want to think out loud, "What would happen to him if Mom and Dad die and something happens to me?" I want to talk about Leyla, who says

Misagh is still the treble clef of her life, that without him she's just a bundle of notes scattered all around in the air with no arrangement. I want to speak about Roja, who wants to leave her mother behind and isn't concerned about it one bit, and that I wish her mother were Mahan's and my mother and that we could go stay with her so none of us would be alone. I want to say all of these things, but Arsalan doesn't like to listen to them. He would turn away and say, "You are such a dreamer," or "What difference does it make?" or "You're too sensitive."

Neither he nor I say anything. Perhaps he too is talking to himself. When he stops the car, I get out. I walk a few steps and look at Tehran, spread out under my feet. The sun is setting, and the lights of the city are turning on one after the other. Each light at each corner is like a star, and in an hour, they form another sky lit up on the ground. The first light is perhaps turned on by an old woman who has weak eyesight. She wants to call her daughter and tell her she does not remember whether the pink pills are for the night or the morning. Maybe the pills are just an excuse. Maybe she just wants to hear her daughter's voice in the deafening silence of the house. The second light is turned on by a little boy whose mother has just left to do some grocery shopping, and who wants to bring the little chicks he has stealthily bought out of the closet and feed them with the handful of millet he has stolen from the store around the corner. The third one perhaps belongs to the night guard of a hospital who has just woken up and, with his puffy eyes, has turned the light on to grab the last piece of bread from his empty fridge and is chewing it while putting on his uniform in order to not be late for his shift at the hospital on the other side of the city. Meanwhile, someone, out of who knows what spite, tells the guard's mother that she delayed asking his cousin's hand in marriage for him for so long that eventually the young mechanic around the corner came and married her, and now he is old and left with no wife. I shove my hands into my pockets and turn toward Arsalan. He doesn't say anything. It's as if he doesn't want to talk at all tonight. Before we walk to the place where the trees block out the sky, I look up. The sky is blue ahead of me and black behind me.

The park is filled with young men and women who rush up the narrow cobblestone path. It's as if they're not at the park right now and it doesn't make a difference if they go farther down or farther up. It's like they're on an escalator; they pause at some point and the cobblestones keep pushing them forward.

The café in the middle of the square is too empty for a summer evening. "Shall we sit here?" I ask Arsalan.

"Here? No way, we should walk to the café farther up. They have great hookahs."

"I'm tired. I'll run out of breath on the stairs. Why not just sit there on the benches next to the lake and watch the ducks?"

He gets started and walks past other people. He pretends he hasn't heard me. He doesn't care about the stairs because he never gets short of breath. As he pulls me with him, his eyes on the road ahead, he begins nagging, as if he isn't even addressing me.

"You are so lazy! It's because you don't work out enough. From now on I have to take you hiking every Friday. You'll lose weight and it'll be good for your spirits too."

I feel upset again. No matter how much Roja tells me, "You fool, he's trying to be affectionate; he just doesn't know how," I don't buy it. There is no trace of affection in his voice. I want to tell him, "I've had these seven or eight kilos of extra weight and this goddamn belly since the first day you came and asked me out. And I intend to keep it from now on. And it's nobody's business." We walk, and Arsalan keeps talking. He talks about his family, his aunt and his grandmother and his grandfather who is a Rubik's Cube champion and holds a record of I-don't-know-how-many seconds. I see my own grandfather, when his eyes were the only part of his body that moved and he wet his mattress like Mahan did when he was a baby. Arsalan's words turn around in my ears and turn into a buzz. His words begin to escape me even before I can hear them. Since I was a child, I've imagined this was how Mahan heard us, whenever he remained frozen and stared at our faces instead of responding. Arsalan keeps talking, and I see his lips moving. I look at him. I look at his profile and the lively movements of his hands when he speaks. When he looks at me, I smile. He mustn't know that I haven't understood a word of what he has said. He pauses.

"I love it when you smile."

My smile becomes a real one, and I feel my heartbeat racing and my breath going all the way in and out. It's because of the exertion, I know. Just the exertion. I find the courage to ask, "Shall we go back?"

He's become kind. "Sure, whatever you want. Next time we'll go all the way to the café up the hill. Do you want to go have ice cream?"

"Yes, let's."

Two young women in high heels stand by the ice cream stand. They try the different flavors and scream and laugh. I stand aside and look at their thin waistlines and straightened, thick hair that spreads on their shoulders in their gorgeous colors. I run a hand over my own thin and lifeless hair that I can only put up in a ponytail. Both of them have long lashes like Roja, and it's clear that they never worry about their mascara running. Arsalan orders two ice cream cups and lets me choose his scoops too. I tell him to pick blackberry and cantaloupe. The joyfulness of their colors suits him. I pick yogurt and green apple for myself. They have less fat. We get our ice cream and begin to walk down the hill. An old man and woman with white sneakers walk by us. Their hands make fists, and they pump them back and forth with the rhythm of their steps. Two young men sit at the raised stone border around the flowerbed, smoking, their eyes dancing around the women's waists. A girl walks in front of a boy, her hands across her chest. The boy grabs her shoulders and pushes her forward, and they both burst out laughing. We walk out of the park gates. I look at the sky, full of stars. "Do you see Orion? The ones that are in a straight line?" I ask him.

"How do you know?"

"And that one is Ursa Major, but in Tehran's polluted sky, only a few of its stars are visible."

I connect the stars in the sky above us with my finger.

"Be careful!"

He moves me out of the way of a large rock in the middle of the path. We get to the car. The return walk was very short. It's because it was downhill. I know. Just because it was downhill. We get in the car. Arsalan hands me his ice cream and turns on the car. I check my cell phone. Leyla had called, and I missed it.

Arsalan fishes a CD out of the dashboard and a calm music starts to play. I roll the window down. I spread all five fingers in the wind and let it take my hand with it. Arsalan talks about work and his plans for the future, plans that also include me. I close my eyes. I feel as if I'm returning from a boxing match. Kicked around, but calm, and a winner. I'm so calm I could sleep for three days and three nights. Today came to an end too. I should remember to grab my paperwork for the insurance application. I should call Leyla when I get home. It's not a long way home. I hope Mahan is still awake.

THREE

I KEEP TELLING MYSELF, "GET up, Roja, get up," and I can't do it. I had gone out to buy myself some gummy bears and didn't want to go home. Not going back, not going back. Dad shouts, "When can I come home?" Mom replies, "Never." Leyla isn't pregnant. She will never give birth to a three-eyed baby to be raised by Shabaneh. Shabaneh stands in the corner and cries. She has failed her exam. Shabestari throws my documents across the desk. These are not complete. I throw dice. It's a double six. Leyla slams the ace of diamonds on the table. Shabaneh leans against the wall and cries. She doesn't know how to play. She tells me, "Your mother died while you were away." I throw my ticket in the face of the embassy guard. The plane doesn't take off. Somebody hands me a phone; Amir Ali's mother is on the line. She begs, "Please, my son has an exam." I throw the phone against the wall. Its insides scatter all over. I scream.

I'm exhausted. Her husband laughs with yellowed teeth. Ramin cleans up pieces of a broken glass and holds my head to his chest. I ask him, "Does this street never end?" He asks, "When are you coming back?" "I'm not sure. Maybe never."

I really have to get up. That's enough. I had nightmares all night long without even closing my eyes. Mom suggested I have a cup of borage tea, but I didn't. It's not like I'm taking the entrance exam for university. It's just an appointment at the embassy that will be done and over by noon. But I couldn't sleep, even though I went to bed early. Maybe it was because of that. First, I tried to watch a movie, *The Big Lebowski*, for the third time. Then I decided against it. "This is not the time to watch a movie. You have to get up at four thirty," I told myself. I slipped under the covers. I turned to one side first, then to the other. It felt as if the sheets were eating at my skin. I kept sitting up, getting up. I had so many nightmares of sleeping in and not getting to my embassy appointment on time. In the end I couldn't close my eyes until morning. Every time I closed my eyelids, it was as if there were springs underneath them; they jumped up and my eyes remained open, wide open. Yesterday I kept humming Leonard Cohen happily to myself. I mean, this is what happened: I had watched the movie *Quills*, and it made me feel so sick that I had to play Cohen very loud in the car. Since last night the damn song hasn't stopped playing in my head. And since it's all mixed up with *Quills*, Cohen keeps singing, and I keep seeing a nightmare of blood. Blood on walls and prisons and other such nasty things. I wish I could take my brain out and scrub it clean with a brush. Keep scrubbing and scrubbing until what's stuck on it gets washed off and runs down the sink. I can't go on like this. I should sleep.

Why isn't my alarm going off? What if it won't? I could just get up and busy myself with something. Watch something. Read something. It's as if the alarm has to give me permission—it has to ring before I can get up. It's over. It's not my fault I can't sleep. Whatever the time is, I am going to get up and go out. I know my eyelids will be puffy and I'll have dark circles around my eyes. My visa picture will turn out ugly. But so what? To hell with it. What matters is not losing my mind first thing in the morning. I roll over. The kitchen light is on. I can hear water running and the clatter of plates and bowls. Has Mom not slept either? What time is it? I pull out my phone from where I was lying on it. I turn it on. Its light hurts my eyes. The all-white light grows pale, and numbers appear on the screen. Like a photograph being developed in a darkroom. It's still a few minutes to four thirty. I've tossed and turned and sweated all night long, and my sheets are all crumpled and damp. I walk out the bedroom.

Mom is standing at the sink with her back to me. She is washing something I can't see. She is wearing her white nightgown. The one with little blue flowers. And she has tied the waistline with a bow on her back. Ramin bought it for her, that's why she keeps wearing it all the time. She is also wearing my hair clip. I was looking for it. I don't know where she took it from. Last night I wanted to dye my own hair and I thought to myself, "Now that I'm going to make a mess in the bathroom, why not dye Mom's hair as well? Two weeks earlier or later, it doesn't really make a difference." I went and bought a blond color for her. I didn't tell her it was blond, I told her it was her usual brown color. The color was revealed after we washed her hair. She didn't say anything. It really suits her. I want to hug her and get lost in her round belly.

"Good morning, Mom. Why are you already awake?"

I startled her. She rinses the frying pan and puts it on the stove. She doesn't smile and say, "Damn you for frightening me like this!"

Instead she frowns and says, "I couldn't sleep. Hurry up or you'll be late."

"It's still early. I'll get ready in a bit. What a nice hair clip!" She doesn't pay me any attention and pours some oil in the frying pan. She takes a handful of chopped herbs from a bowl next to the stove and adds them to the pan. With her chubby fingers, she turns the spatula around in the pan with no extra effort, as if she has done so since the beginning of time. The scent of dill fills the house and reminds me of our home in Rasht. How am I going to live without Mom?

"Go get dressed. Breakfast will be ready in a moment."

I walk to my room. She doesn't even turn to look at me. I know what's going on. She is on the verge of crying and doesn't want me to see her eyes. Last night she kept insisting that I drink some borage tea to relax. She gave me advice on how to respond to the interview questions. Do this. Don't do this. She wanted me to think she's happy that I'm leaving. But I'm not stupid; I know that deep in her heart, she wants something to go wrong so I can't leave. She had said, "Go ahead and leave, but what am I going to do all by myself?"

I had just put the grocery bags on the floor. It was during my second year in college. Mom had not yet gotten used to living in Tehran. I had bought a dozen eggs, fifty flatbreads, two kilos of chicken, and a lot of fruit. The bags were so heavy my arms were about to fall off. I asked her if we had rice.

"Didn't you say you were only going to be away for four days? Why did you buy so much stuff?"

She was right. The Tabriz camping trip was only four days, but I had shopped for two weeks. The trip was organized by the university. We were going to visit the Iran Tractor Manufacturing Company. Everyone was going. Shabaneh, Leyla, Misagh, Hamed. Leyla had not yet married Misagh. She just loved him. Misagh had invited her to a reading, and we had gone along. She still hadn't told him anything. She couldn't bring herself to do so. I knew Misagh from our film club. Leyla had asked me to go with her to the reading to talk and joke around so that Misagh would become friends with our group. "Do you think I'm a clown?" I had retorted, and added, "What should I do with Mom?" "Why? Isn't Ramin there?" she had asked. Ramin was not home. He had gone to Rasht to stay with Grandma—Auntie Fakhri had had a stroke. That time, it didn't matter to me that Mom would be on her own. I was tired of rushing home every day to be there for Mom. I wanted to travel like everyone. I wasn't supposed to be Mom's mom. I had saved the money for the trip myself. Mom had told me to go. I had packed my things and gone shopping. I had told her, "What's the problem? We'll have enough food for two or three weeks . . . just, for God's sake, don't leave the bread out. It's not humid here like in Rasht. It'll get stale immediately."

I was worried that, left alone, she would once again forget that the weather here was dry and the bread would go stale. She didn't go shopping in Tehran. She struggled with the stairs because of her herniated disc and she didn't know her way around. She didn't know where the shops were, and I was worried she would get lost. Her real problem wasn't groceries—learned that during that trip. When we arrived in Tabriz, I called her with Leyla's cell phone. She said she had run out of yogurt. The following day she said she had been so scared that she had not slept at all—there were noises coming from the neighbor's house. That night I couldn't sleep. I kept having a nightmare that the lions of the Saravan Forest were ripping her apart, and I wouldn't reach her. Every half an hour I would wake up with a jolt. Eventually I got up and called Grandma's house from the hotel lobby and told Ramin to go back to Tehran. "Why are you crying? I'll get on the road now," he said. And he returned home.

Last night I decided that I won't have any bad thoughts today. I kept telling myself that it was not my fault that Mom would be left on her own. It was not my fault that Dad had died. I sit in front of my vanity and do my hair. I'm still not used to having short hair. Having quarreled with my pillow all night long, every strand of my hair is pointing in a different direction. They are not easily tamed. I need to iron them.

I should not be sad. I should be thankful for the life I have. A lot of people envy it. I should think about good things. I should think about my life in France—about walking on its streets, about its movie theaters, about graduating with a PhD in five years, about my admission and the scholarship I've won, about the university and the head of the mechanical engineering department who wrote me that he would be honored for me to attend his class. If these aren't all reasons for happiness, then what is?

Didn't I sit with her that very first day to explain my situation and ask her, "Mom, what should I do?" Didn't she herself say, "You should improve your life. Don't think about me"? Didn't she say, "I'm so proud of you. I'll never stop you," and other things like that? Now what's with her face and all? She hasn't looked at me at all this morning. I had said, "Didn't you come to Tehran just because of me? When I go to France, you won't have any more reasons to stay here. You can go back to Rasht."

She was changing the sheets on Ramin's bed. I had said, "You won't have to rent anymore. You'll go back to your own house. And if your sister can check in with you every week, that would be great."

"I don't have anyone in Rasht."

"Isn't Auntie anyone?"

"My next of kin is not my sister. You are here, Ramin is here."

"But I won't be here anymore."

"Ramin will be here."

Ramin is not here. He is doing his residency all the way in Dehloran. And when he gets back, how much time can he really spend with her? When he starts working, he will have to do long shifts. She has to get used to spending the nights on her own eventually. Isn't that just how the world works? For thousands of years, children have left the nest. For thousands of years, mothers have stayed behind on their own. I need to break free from Mom at some point. I should stop thinking that she might be sad, might get lost, might break her leg, might have a stroke. I cannot stay with her forever. All these people who've left, they haven't died of heartbreak, nor have their mothers. Maybe, as Shabaneh suggests, we should just get a house and put Mom and Mahan in it to live together, so neither of them is alone.

My hair isn't really coming together. I had asked Ms. Nazanin to cut it in a way that I could style a few different ways. She suggested that whenever I wasn't in the mood to style my hair, I could just let it fall on my forehead. I do just that. At least this way I don't have to worry about it falling out of shape under my scarf by the time I get to the embassy. When I pick up the hair spray I hear Mom calling, "Roja, breakfast."

She has set the table. She pretends to be busy with sweetening her tea and putting spoons by the plates. There is tea, milk, dates, and sunny-side-up eggs with dill. The other day she had called to ask me to get some dill on my way home.

"With your backache, you want to sit and clean dill?"

"We need it. Get us some."

She sat and cleaned the whole bunch. Then she spread the herb on a sheet on the living room floor and turned on the fan over them. And afterward she kept saying she had a backache. "Didn't I tell you not to do that?" The following day she gave me a jar full of dried dill. "You should take this with you when you leave. You might want to make baghali ghatogh or sabzi polo or something, if you have guests," she said. "Mom, what are you talking about? Do you think I'll have time to cook? And if the jar opens, the dill will just spread all around my suitcase and ruin my clothes."

"What's the occasion for such an elaborate breakfast?"

She doesn't respond. The toast jumps up in the toaster. Mom bundles it in the red checkered cotton cloth and puts it in the bread basket. During breakfast she continues to sulk. I keep telling myself that I too should sulk and not eat, but I don't have the courage. It'll break her heart. And who knows, maybe this is the last time I'll have a homemade breakfast like this. Who is going to serve me breakfast on the first day of school in France? And I won't find dill there. Even if I take the dried dill with me, who is going to be in the mood to moisten dried dill early in the morning? I might even have to skip breakfast to get to class on time. Mom's breakfast paints the morning with colors, it's such a good start to the day. This breakfast is a breakfast of important occasions. The days of finals, the first day of high school, the day of Ramin's entrance exam, and most importantly the day of the national university exam. That day I had the same breakfast. Then I went to the session and poured my brain onto the paper. I filled so many white boxes until the checkered multiple choice test paper, like King Solomon's flying carpet, brought Mom and me from Rasht to Tehran.

"What a pity you cut your beautiful hair."

"I have to study hard in France and I have to work too. Where would I find the time to style long hair?"

She gives me a bite of bread and egg.

"Besides, my room won't have a private bathroom. Washing that much wavy hair will give me so much trouble. And how will I untangle the knots when you aren't there?"

She remains silent. I'm really not in the mood for this sad vibe.

"You know, one has to have good luck. What does hair really matter, in the greater scheme of things?

She doesn't even smile. She makes this amazing breakfast and then goes ahead and ruins it completely with her sulking. Has she forgotten that when I was admitted, she sat by the phone for two days and showed off to everyone who called that her daughter was accepted to a PhD program in France? Well, she had also cried, because she would be left all by herself. She had said, "First my husband's fate, now my children." But deep down she had been happy.

"I didn't add any garlic, so you can eat it. Aren't you going to be late?"

"I've arranged for the taxi to be here at five fifteen. Even that is too early."

"You're not taking your own car?"

"No, the embassy is in the traffic congestion zone and I don't want to get a ticket."

I pour some milk in my tea to cool it. I drink it all in one gulp. Taking big mouthfuls helps one swallow big worries.

"Thanks, Mom."

"Why didn't you eat anything?"

"I did. I just ate fast. I'm full."

I get up and call the taxi. He says he remembers he has to pick me up and will be there in twenty minutes. Last night Leyla said she could pick me up, but I declined. "Why would you do that? You haven't been sleeping well. Why wake up so early just to come pick me up? Your whole day will be ruined. They wouldn't even let you come into the embassy with me, anyway." She told me I could borrow her car, as it has the permit for the traffic zone. I told her no. "You need to go to the newsroom yourself." Finally, she said that she would wake me up. She didn't. She hasn't woken up herself, perhaps. I knew she would sleep in. She dreams of Misagh all night. I should take her with me to France. Samira is there too. That would do her good.

I sit at my vanity. My hair and my brows look good. I just have dark circles under my eyes. I pick the concealer and rub it around my eyes. Now I look as if I've slept like a baby all night long. I don't wear eyeliner. I look more natural like this. I put on brown eye shadow and mascara. My eyes come to life. I put on my glasses. I draw in my cheeks. Dad used to say, "Roja, turn into a fish." I drew in my cheeks. When the goldfish inside the bowl said, "Daddy, daddy," I said it too. Grandma said, "You're spoiling this kid, Mohsen."

I put on my blush in the curves of my cheeks. My face looks steady and strong. When Shabestari sees me, she'll know how confident I am about leaving. I just need to put on my lipstick. I choose a light color. Europeans don't put on too much makeup. I pick my brown shirt from the hanger and cut off the price tag. I had asked the salesman whether its color would be resistant in the sun. "Won't you be wearing it under your manteau? How would the sun reach it?" he had retorted. Shabaneh told him I would be wearing it without a manteau, in France. I will wear it on my first day on campus. It's simple and chic, which is good for a foreign student. They wouldn't think that I'm provincial, excited to finally wear whatever I want. Its English spread collar will look nice in photographs. The only thing that looks shabby is my manteau. It's gotten old. Last night when I was ironing it, Mom said, "You should get a new one. Don't keep walking around with these shabby ones." "Why should I buy a new one? I'll be leaving in a few weeks. What use do I have for a manteau anymore?" I replied.

"Don't you want one to go to the embassy?" she asked. "I'll take my manteau off there," I explained. Mom doesn't know that no one wears a manteau on the embassy grounds.

I walk back to the living room. I check myself out in the tall mirror. I look nice. Mom isn't there. She's gone back to bed. I walk back to my room and grab the red folder and my purse. I notice the DVDs spread on my desk. Leyla had asked me to lend her some movies to watch at night. She said she wanted something to take her mind off things when she got home from work. I look through them quickly and put a few in my purse. "Bye, Mom," I shout.

She is standing by the door of her room.

"Be well. Don't worry. It'll all turn out fine."

Our eyes lock for a second, and that second freezes and becomes many hours. I force my gaze away and get out of the house.

The taxi is waiting for me downstairs. A black Peugeot with a young, sleepy driver at the wheel. I wait for a while, but he doesn't start the car.

"Didn't they tell you? I'm going to the French Embassy. On Neauphle-le-Château Street."

"Under Hafez Overpass?"

"Yes." Whatever I say in Farsi, I repeat to myself in French as well. I keep testing myself; I'm so worried that I'll arrive in France and want to say something but fail to find the words. I keep practicing in my head. I imagine taking a cab in France. I want to go to the Iranian Embassy to renew my passport. The car is a black Peugeot exactly like this one, but the driver is a Black man, like the Black man in *Requiem for a Dream*, except that he's a good person. I tell him, "*Bonjour Monsieur, Avenue d'Iéna, s'il vous plaît.*" He asks me if I'm a foreigner. I say yes. "You speak French very well," he observes. "You don't have an accent at all." Then he asks me whether I had learned French in my own country, and I proudly say yes. And then I might feel homesick for the alleys of Vila Street.

"Are you moving for school?"

The driver is looking at me in the rearview mirror with shiny red eyes.

"Yes, I was admitted to college."

"It's so strange that everybody is leaving these days. My cousin left last week."

He taps on the steering wheel with his palm several times.

"Why shouldn't you leave? What good is it staying here?"

Misagh drew a hand over his forehead.

"Am I lying, Roja? What will she do if she stays? All of us. Why should we stay here?"

Mom left the tea tray on the table. Misagh said, "Can you talk her into it? I swear to God I don't want to leave without her. Take my word for it. She is leaving me no choice."

Man that he was, he was on the verge of crying. What had nasty Leyla done to him? Always well-groomed and well-dressed, Misagh had showed up at our house with a T-shirt full of stains to ask me and Mom for help. "It would be a pity to leave your life, my son. Can't you just stay here and continue with your studies?" Mom asked.

"I can't. If I stay, I won't be satisfied with my life. I know myself too well. I don't want to go to work right away. I hate having a boss. There's nothing left for me here. Leaving would offer me a new world. I keep telling Leyla, 'Let's go. If we can't stay, if you don't like it there, we can always come back.' She won't agree. It's such a shame. I was admitted to college, fully funded. Why should I stay here?"

If he hadn't left, he would have regretted it. His life would be destroyed. And he would hate Leyla for having held him back. I will regret it too if I don't leave. Then, years from now, I would sit with myself, exactly like this driver, and sigh. Wouldn't I tell myself, "Roja, wouldn't your life be better if you had left?" Wouldn't I be filled with envy? I would. I'm sure of it. That envy would not let me live anymore. It would not let me be happy. It would devour all my joys. It would crush me completely.

"When you get there, don't forget about us, the miserable ones. Be well."

I get out of the car. What's going on here this early in the morning? It's still dark. Why all the people, then? All the cars? Half the people are asleep in their cars. Have they been here since last night? The rest are standing in line, folders in hand. These folders are our King Solomon's carpets. They'll pick us up and take us to France. I wasn't very focused this morning. What if I've left something behind? These documents have been driving me insane. Mom said, "Stop spreading them around on the floor and gathering them up over and over again. You'll end up losing one." I said I wouldn't lose any. But what if I have? I open my folder and browse quickly through the papers. The letter of admission; the fucking six-thousand-euro payment slip; translations of my birth certificate, my transcripts, my diplomas, my job proof, the deed of our house in Rasht, and the lease contract of our house in Tehran; my passport, which is valid for five years; my handwritten personal statement; and my language test scores. I've arranged their copies in order as well. Nothing is missing. I've checked them ten times since last night.

I'm becoming obsessed like Grandma. Whenever she comes to Tehran, she calls Auntie Fakhri three times every day and asks her to check the stove to make sure it's turned off, turn up the air conditioner, and lock the door. Even with all that, she wakes up in the middle of the night, worried that a burglar might have strangled Auntie Fakhri. Two days later, she goes back to Rasht, and Mom breathes a sigh of relief. Someone taps me on the shoulder.

"You need to put your name on the list. Add it to the list in that guy's hand. We'll be let in based on the order of the list."

I look where he's pointing. A middle-aged man with a piece of paper in his hand stands on the other side of the fences by the gate. A cluster of people surrounds him. They don't let me through easily. I push my way through men in suits and women in makeup. I reach the man. He is fat, and I imagine the sweat on his forehead must have something to do with it being so busy at this cool hour of the early morning.

"Would you please write down my name too?"

"What's your name?"

I'm the twenty-sixth person. I woke up at four in the morning and I'm still the twenty-sixth? When did these other people wake up to come stand in line? Mom hates lines. Bakery line. Bank line. Milk line. When we were kids, she would go stand in the milk line very early in the morning. She wouldn't let Ramin go. She would bring home the cheap milk and make cheap yogurt with it. I always eyed her shopping bag to see if she had bought us chocolate milk. She never did. It was bad for us. Regular milk was better. It was always Grandma who brought us chocolate milk. When she came to our house to bring us Dad's share from the store sales. She would bring us bananas too, so that we would grow strong and study well. When

Ramin was admitted into medical school, Auntie said it was because of the bananas. Mom got upset.

After Grandma left, Mom would always take me and Ramin to the City Hall Square. We would walk around and have ice cream. She would buy pencils for Ramin and dolls for me. Then we would go to Jahangir to have kebab. The best days of our lives were those days. I don't know what day of the week it was. They were better than Thursdays, when Mom would make chicken or cutlet sandwiches early in the morning and then take me and Ramin to Tazeh Abad to visit Dad's grave. She used to say we were all together on those days. We would sit there together all day until it got dark. Mom didn't cry anymore. She had run out of tears. She would throw a blanket next to the stone slab of his tomb. She would sit down and watch me and Ramin. We would play hopscotch over the tombstones. Ramin could already read, and he would read me the engravings on the gravestones. We would compete—Ramin could jump over three tombstones. I couldn't jump more than two, no matter how hard I tried. I would cheat and stand half a step forward on the first tombstone and then jump. Nobody ever found out.

I feel disoriented behind these closed gates. I ask the man who has jotted down my name, "Why did you make a list? We could just stand in line."

"The doors open at seven thirty. Until then you can go wherever you want."

Where could I possibly go at this early hour? If Leyla had come with me, we could go have breakfast. I'm really craving the omelets we used to buy near campus. But for now, I need to hold on to my purse and folder and sit on the curb.

I had been sitting on the curb and had my purse and folder on my lap. I twisted my long hair with my fingers and let it go, staring at the windows of the houses along the street. It was almost sunset. I had been sitting there since dawn. I had wanted to go upstairs ten times, but I had been too scared. I didn't know how to tell Mom about my letter of admission. I had provided the university with the company's address. The letter had arrived that morning. Shabaneh was next to me when I opened it. I felt wild with joy. I went outside several times and came back in. Then I started pacing around the office. Nothing could calm me down. My joy was overflowing. My head could not contain it. I felt like I was suffocating. I opened the window and took a deep breath all the way into my lungs and bent over outside toward the persimmon tree. Shabaneh grabbed my waist and pulled me back in. "Are you crazy? You'll fall down." I hugged her and held her tight. When I let her go, she sat down on my chair and began to cry. "Why are you crying? You'll still have Leyla. Everyone will be with you here. It's me who's leaving and will be all by myself over there. See how I'm not crying?" I said.

"You never cry. You're not afraid of being alone. You're not afraid of anything. You'll leave and not even take one last glance behind you. Also, those who stay behind and don't accompany us all the way are not true friends."

I didn't know where she had read that. A little while later, I started to think of all the hardships. I called Leyla. "How should I break the news to Mom?" I asked her. She started joking. "You should all go to hell. You're all leaving." She said, "It's not Imam Khomeini. It's really Behesht-e Zahra Cemetery. It takes everyone from me." She said, "You too should go and be happy. Leave us here all on our own." She said, "You'll go and there'll be an earthquake here and we'll all die. Then you'll regret having left." She kept talking and laughing. But deep down her laughter was bitter and full of sorrow. It was as if she were running out of breath at the end of each word. I was nervous. For the first time in ages, I felt like crying. I wasn't sure whether it was of joy or sadness. I felt like my heart would crack in half from feeling both simultaneously, the way a crystal glass would crack if you poured hot and cold water into it, one immediately after the other.

The last step still remained. Mom. She opened my bedroom window and scattered bread crumbs on the sill so that the pigeons would come eat them and make noise, so she would not feel sad and lonely. I knew after that she would go to the kitchen and put the rice pot on the stove, and fifteen minutes later the scent of fresh Lahijan rice would fill the apartment. Ramin was supposed to come home that night from Dehloran. It had gotten dark. I was tired of sitting on the curb. I thought to myself, Fuck it. I have to tell her eventually. The sooner I tell her, the sooner I'll be relieved. I didn't ring the buzzer and opened the door with my own keys. I took my time going up the stairs, one step at a time. I could feel my arms and legs dragging on the floor, as if I were a child again and had gotten a bad grade in school. When I opened the door, I was welcomed by the scent of fried garlic and grilled eggplants.

"Hi, Mom. Oh, you look so beautiful!"

She had taken a shower and was wearing makeup. She was wearing her hair up in a topknot bun. She was in a very good mood, so good that I didn't feel like ruining it for her.

"Of course. My son is coming home tonight. He'll arrive any minute. Wait a while so we can have dinner together."

"We always have to wait for your one-of-a-kind son!"

I wish I had waited for Ramin to get home. The two of us could have come upstairs together. Then he would say something, and I would say something, and the whole thing would be over somehow.

I put my folder on the table. I stood over it for half an hour and kept wanting to say something, but the words were stuck at the bottom of my throat and swirled around in my head. I was tired of all those scattered sentences that sounded more or less the same. I went to my room. Mom's voice came through the door.

"Will you go buy some yogurt, Roja? I've made some dalal herbs for Ramin. And get your folder out of here. I want to set the dinner table."

I gathered all my strength to say, "I left it there on purpose. It's the letter from the university."

I couldn't believe it was my voice coming from my throat. It sounded different. It was as if I were stuck in between the plates of a press. I hated this life. Even its joys are complicated. I waited in the darkness of the bedroom. Mom's round body moved into the light of the doorframe. She held the folder in her hand and stared at me like a statue. I said everything quite fast, so it would be done as soon as possible.

"I've been accepted for a PhD in Toulouse. It's kind of in the south of France. Like where Shiraz is in Iran. I have to be there in two months at the latest."

She turned the light on. She came into my room and embraced me. She said she was proud of me. She said she had the best daughter in the world, who was worth her whole life. She said we needed to celebrate.

"Wonderful, so my plans for summer holidays are all set then. I'll tell everyone I'm going to visit my daughter in Paris."

I didn't tell her it was several hours by train from Toulouse to Paris. I didn't tell her I had no money to have fun in Paris. I didn't tell her that even if she set aside Dad's pension for the next ten years, it wouldn't be enough to buy a plane ticket. I didn't say that I didn't know when I could even get enough money for a ticket to come back home for a visit. I decided to let her be happy. It's easier to deal with bad news if you hear it little by little. Instead, I began teasing her. I made her laugh. I told her to not hold her breath, that my apartment would be pretty small and she would have to go to a hotel. She said even if she did go to a hotel, I had to take her out every day. I had to show her all around Paris. We talked. We laughed. I could hear her laughter when I suddenly noticed her shoulders. They were trembling. I held her face in my hands. It was soaking wet.

"Numbers one to ten, line up along the fence. The gate is going to open soon."

It is as if someone has turned a hose on an ant colony. Everyone has started to run around. What's going on? We'll all get in eventually. Our names are on the list. A few people go stand on the other side of the fence. Others go and wake those sleeping in their cars. They get up and, with puffy, alarmed eyes, run to find their spot among the people on the other side. They seem to be gloating from their vantage point over those of us still waiting our turn behind the fence. They look as if they've won a competition or something. It's still a long while till it's my turn. I don't have the energy to move from my spot at the curb. I look up at the people around me as if I'm a child with Mom and Dad and Ramin at the bazaar, where we've come to buy Mom some earrings. Mom's earrings were diamond-shaped with three shades of gold. She used to tell everyone they were made in Italy.

When Dad died, she sold them. She sold all the gold she had. She didn't like accepting money from Grandma. She still doesn't like it. She said Dad died because of the store, so she didn't want Dad's share from the store's income. Grandma came to our house every day. She cried. She left the money under the carpet. She told Mom how much she loved her. She swore on Ramin's and my life that Dad's death had nothing to do with the store. She said Naser Khan's body would tremble in the grave if Mohsen's children were going through a tough time. My grandfather wasn't really a khan. He was a grocer. I don't know why his last name was Khan. The first time I got paid for tutoring, I bought Mom a pair of diamond-shaped earrings. Exactly like those she had sold.

"Are you also here for a student visa?"

I turn around. It's a young woman who looks like Catherine Deneuve. She is short but is wearing high heels. She's wearing red lipstick and has her long black hair loose under her thin headscarf. How much time did she spend blow-drying her hair?

"Yes. You too?"

"Yes, me too."

Her cell phone buzzes. She excuses herself and walks away.

Leyla had said, "Me too." I didn't have a problem with that at all. No. I was deeply happy that among all the guys, I had finally found a woman. Now, if Ramin asked me in the evening whether I had made any friends on campus, I could say yes. But I was convinced that no other girl would have the courage to choose mechanical engineering as her major. Now I was irritated that this delicate girl, with light brown hair, thin, groomed eyebrows, and chic clothes, was standing there telling me she too had been accepted for mechanical engineering. I thought I was done for and that from then on I would have to take care of all the lathing and welding projects for her. I let her go in front of me to take the picture for her ID card.

"Are you from Tehran?" I asked her.

"No, I'm from Ahwaz."

"So why are you so light-skinned?"

"Not everyone from Ahwaz is dark-skinned."

They told us we needed to go to the registration office at the school of engineering and handed us a large map so that we wouldn't get lost on that huge campus. As we began walking there together, I asked her, "Why did you choose mechanical engineering?"

"No good reason. If I have to study engineering, what difference does it make what major I choose? They're all the same."

"Did you want to study something else?"

"Yes, music."

"But mechanical engineering is super technical. We'll end up having to work in factories."

"It's not like that. We'll all end up at desk jobs, signing plans."

I thought it would be impossible to have fun with this girl. She wouldn't be up for anything. I figured I'd have to get myself a different friend.

The campus seemed endless. No matter how much we walked, we never arrived at the school of engineering. Leyla followed me nonchalantly, as if she had always been a college student, while I kept asking everyone for directions, as if I were a recently released prisoner who hadn't seen people for a long time. I don't know why I was so excited. For the brick buildings with cold light blue walls? For the battered classroom chairs? For the tall, skinny guys with glasses and half-grown beards who wore their crumpled shirts loose over their trousers, or the girls who looked like they were still in high school?

"Where are you from?" she asked.

"I'm from Rasht."

"Will you be staying at the dorm?"

"No, my mom is going to move to Tehran; we're renting a place."

"Good for you. I have to live in the dorms. My father doesn't like the idea of me renting a place on my own."

The school of engineering felt welcoming. The building was full of seniors who had come over to help us choose our credits. They told us to go to the computer lab and wait for them. A chubby girl with a long navy blue manteau and full eyebrows was standing, confused, by the lab door. She held her backpack to her chest with one hand and chewed the nails of her other hand. She looked like she was going to burst into tears at any moment. I asked her, "Are you also a mechanical engineering freshman?"

She lowered her hand and said yes. Her eyes kept moving back and forth between my face and Leyla's. I told her we were too. She looked as if we had offered her the whole world. Her face muscles relaxed. "Do you know where the restrooms are?" she asked in a low voice.

"No. You could've asked the secretary."

"I was too shy."

"What is there to be shy about? Did you already choose your credits?"

"I don't know how to do that."

Holding back her tears, she then turned her head a bit to the left and cautiously showed us the corner of her headscarf without saying a word. A sparrow had left its mark. Leyla told her that it didn't matter, that nobody would see it.

I said, "What do you mean it doesn't matter? It's sloppy to go around like that on the first day of college. All the guys will make fun of her." I went and asked the secretary where the restroom was. The girl washed her scarf. She was about to put it back on when I stopped her. I loosened her hair from her ponytail. I combed her bangs with my fingers and brushed them out to the side on her forehead. What kind of a look was that? On her first day of college she had made herself look like a schoolgirl. The night before, Mom and I had spent two hours cleaning up my eyebrows.

"You look great now! By the way, what's your name?" Leyla asked her.

"Shabaneh."

"What a strange name. Where are you from?"

"I'm from Tehran. My dad loves Shamlou. He named me after the title of one of his poems. Where are you two from?"

Leyla pointed at me. "Roja is from Rasht. I'm from Ahwaz."

"Why are you so light-skinned, then?"

Leyla and I laughed. Shabaneh asked, "Can we choose our credits together, so we get to be classmates?"

"Sure. I just can't do eight o'clock classes. I won't be able to get up on time," said Leyla.

"Me neither!" I agreed.

A voice says, "Numbers ten to twenty on the list, get in line."

The girl who looks like Catherine Deneuve takes a step forward. With her high heels, she walks like a Japanese geisha. Why does she do this to herself? Any moment now she could trip and fall down. I get up and hold her arm so she can step over the gutter.

"Thank you, darling. See you later."

I'm starting to feel sleepy, but the city is just waking up. You can see Hafez Overpass from the end of Neauphle-le-Château Street. There is traffic and a lot of noise from the horns and all the cars. The people lining up in front of the embassy gate have tripled. Do all these people want to go to France? A man arrives and shouts, "Travel insurance . . ." Two women walk to him. They negotiate. Then they walk together to the alley on the side. Should I buy travel insurance too? I really don't have any money left for that. Once again, I look at the documents. They don't say anything about insurance. I might not need it, then. The girl who looks like Catherine Deneuve has gone inside. I look around for someone who might be a student to double-check with him. One can easily recognize the students. They are younger and simpler and they stand all by themselves. And the folders they're holding are larger.

"Numbers twenty to thirty, line up at the gate."

I forget about asking around. Even if I need insurance, I can't do anything about it now. The crowd doesn't let me pass. I utter a dozen "excuse-mes" to make my way to the gate. I ask the numbers of everyone in line. They see me going from one to the other and asking, but none of them offers to help and tell me where my spot is. I find the twenty-fifth person. She is an old woman with a white manteau and a pink satin headscarf. I stand behind her and look behind me. There's a young man who looks like a student.

"What's your number?"

"Twenty-seven."

"So you're standing in the right spot. Are you here for a student visa as well?"

"Yes."

"Do we also need to have travel insurance?"

"I don't think so."

He looks down. He is shy. He is like Ramin, who hides when he meets a stranger, covering himself with a metal sheet like RoboCop. Mom says, "My son is a girl and my daughter a boy. They should have switched places." Ramin had hidden under the balcony stairs. I was playing tag with the kids in the courtyard when I saw him. Uncle had brought him home early from school. He had gone under the stairs and hadn't come out. He had hugged his knees and kept staring at the corner of the yard. I looked in that direction too but there was nothing there. I was happy we had so many guests. The sound of my playing and laughing was drowned out by Mom's and Aunt Fakhri's wails. Grandma wept. "Mohsen, Mohsen, I knew one day you would lose your life for your cause," she cried out. Mom came to the balcony. Her hair was disheveled. Her lips were white. Two black lines went from under her eyes to her chin. When the kids saw her, they retreated to a corner of the courtyard and stood silently in a row. As if Mom was to be feared. She called me. She seemed to have lost her voice. Like people who suffer a cold. Two or three times she opened her mouth, but no voice came out, until finally she was able to mutter her question. Had I seen Ramin? I didn't dare say he was hiding. He might have done something wrong. I said I hadn't seen him. Mom came downstairs. She wasn't wearing her slippers. Her bare feet tap-tapped over the mosaics of the courtyard. She called Ramin several times. He didn't respond. I joined her in calling.

"Ramin, Ramin!"

Aunt Fakhri came to the balcony and let out a scream. "Where is your father, Ramin?"

Dad had gone to Manjil to buy supplies for Grandpa's grocery store. He had not brought back supplies. He had died. He had died young. Only his green eyes remained, and my fish imitations. Just that. Mom saw Ramin under the staircase. She picked him up. She unlocked his arms. She put them around her waist. They both cried. I ran toward them. I hugged Mom's legs from behind. I too started to cry.

If I had drunk that borage tea last night, I would not be thinking these thoughts now. I am worried, so I keep having bad thoughts. I have to think about something else.

"What is your major?" I ask the shy student with number twenty-seven.

"Computer science. But I was admitted to photography."

"Interesting! I have a friend whose major was mechanical engineering, like me, but she loves music. As much as we tried, she wouldn't come to work at this company where another friend of ours and I got jobs."

He looks down. He doesn't care what Leyla studied or what she likes. I wonder how, with this shyness of his, he is going to talk to Shabestari. The woman in front of me takes two steps forward and one step down. She passes the metal gate. An old man with a cane stands in front of me. This system has enslaved people. Couldn't they schedule interviews in a humane manner so that such an old man isn't obliged to stand in line for so long? I've arrived at one end of the fence. The man who wrote down people's names is gone. In his stead, a young man has come, with muscular arms and a thick silver necklace. Shabaneh should be here. She loves muscles. Crazy girl. I look at the paper in the young man's hand. He jots down the number one hundred and twelve. The one hundred and twelfth person is a young woman who keeps begging him to let her go inside. Her appointment was at nine thirty. She didn't know she had to come early. How sloppy people can be! How could she not know that she had to come early? A dozen people had told me I needed to come and wait in line starting at six in the morning. Even if they hadn't, how could I have calmly stayed at home until the time of my appointment?

In front of the woman, there is a revolving door with beige bars. She pushes them. The door revolves. The bars get locked behind her with a loud sound. I pass through the metal gate. I remain behind the bars. I hear someone screaming outside. A woman shouts and asks why a man from the travel agency has brought ten people with him to the line. The man swears he has written all the names on the list. Their voices grow louder and louder. Even when I arrive in France I won't be freed of these people. Someone from inside gestures that I can go through. When I push the bars, I enter another world. A strange, cool world. The voice of the old man with the cane, who's saying it's the same story here every day, gets lost.

A few steps farther, a frowning man sits behind the glass in a kiosk. He stares at me. Guessing at what he wants, I hand him my passport. He keeps staring at me.

"What?" I ask.

"Your letter of admission."

Why didn't you just say so? How should I know? I don't have divine powers. I pass my letter of admission under the opening in the glass. He looks at it. He posts a piece of paper on my passport. He jots down the number three on it. I take my passport back. There is another door in front of me. This place looks like the cave of Ali Baba and the forty thieves of Baghdad. I have to pass through ten doors. I open another. There is a French guard behind a glass door. On the pocket of his blue short-sleeve shirt, I read SÉCURITÉ. I read the words on the glass. I have to hand in my cell phone and my keys. I take out my cell phone. I turn it off. I put my keys next to it. I pass them under the glass. I put my purse and my folder on the tray of the X-ray machine. The SÉCURITÉ checks my cell phone. He smiles at me. I feel like talking to him. I thank him profusely in French. He seems to like it. He wishes me luck. I walk out of the glass room.

In front of me, there is a hall with wooden walls. It is full of people. I stand in a corner. People yawn. They keep staring at each other. I wonder what they keep searching for in one another's faces. Nobody talks to anybody. It seems as if they are all preparing themselves for exile. At the end of the hall, I see Catherine Deneuve.

There is an empty chair next to her. She takes her purse so that I can sit. She grabs my passport and looks at it.

"That number is for students. The first person just went in. I am the second one."

She points to a large wooden door on the left. As I sit down, the shy guy enters the hall. When he sees me, he comes toward me. He looks confused, like he's wondering whether he should say something. He doesn't. He sits in the row behind us. I tell Catherine Deneuve that he is a student too. She turns and smiles at him. Who knows? Maybe we can all become friends here.

I let my headscarf down over my shoulders. I wrap it once around my neck. I take my mirror out of my purse. The scarf looks good. I arrange my hair. Catherine Deneuve grabs my mirror. She looks at herself.

"My hair looks bad. Do you know what questions they will ask?"

"I've heard they ask why you want to go to France, why you've chosen your major, and other questions like that."

She opens her purse and takes out a makeup bag, a very large one. She freshens her red lipstick.

"I've memorized my answers. I'm afraid if they ask something else, I won't know what to answer."

"Don't worry. The questions aren't hard. What's important is that the university has already admitted you. Shabestari, the woman who's in charge of the students' files, only checks the documents."

"By the way, did you get a receipt?"

I haven't. She shows me the kiosk. A few people stand in front of it, money in hand. I wait for my turn. A bald man wearing a red tie sits at the register. When I give him my money and passport, he hands me a receipt. I put it in my red folder, over my papers. I walk back. I tell the shy guy to go get a receipt. He doesn't speak with anyone. In the end, he goes in without having gotten the receipt. I sit next to Catherine Deneuve again. Not that I like her, no. I talk to pass the time. She chews her words before speaking them. I hear only half of them. Her name is Sayeh. She is five years younger than me. She has just finished her studies and has been admitted for biology. She says her father insisted that she go to Paris for her studies because that's where her uncle lives. As we get to know each other a bit more, she looks around, then quietly confesses that she paid a lawyer four million tomans to get her an admission.

"Four million tomans? What the hell? Why didn't you do it yourself?"

A woman with honey-colored, styled hair, wearing a skirt and a blouse, comes out of the side door. She is around forty years old. She is Shabestari. I recognize her from what I have heard of her. From her frowning. From her holding her head and chest up when she walks. And from her not looking at anyone.

"Number two. Come in and close the door behind you."

She goes back inside. Sayeh gets up. She walks in, her high heels clicking on the floor.

I am still thinking about the four million tomans she paid the lawyer. How many eighty thousand tomans equals four million tomans? Fifty. It means tutoring five new students, each for ten sessions. Or working at the company for four months, from eight to five.

Shabaneh said, "They've said they'll hire me full-time, so I won't continue and do a master's. I'm tired of studying. I want to go to work. They need more people. Do you want to come too?"

We had just completed our finals. Shabaneh had already worked for them part-time. They had promised to hire her full-time when she finished her studies. At first, I thought to myself that she was right, it would be best to start working right away. I would be an engineer, and everyone, including me, would breathe in a sigh of relief. But I wasn't convinced. A path unspooled in front of me that could be blocked by work, like a full stop bringing everything to an end. I said, "I can't, Shabaneh. I can't put my heart in it. I want to get my master's. I'll come to work after that."

"But you don't even like studying."

I didn't like studying, but I couldn't stop thinking about university. Something kept bugging me, something like avarice, like envy. Not that I was a jealous person. No. But it seemed like I was competing with myself, with anyone who had a master's degree. Later, when I finished my master's, I felt like I had been pulled too far away by the waves. The master's didn't feel like enough. I still had to check emigrating and getting a PhD off my list. It was like a game. With each level complete, the next level would open up in front of me. My dreams just felt like a mirage. Even before I had achieved one thing, I began to desire something else. I had to leave Iran. There was no other choice. Shabaneh's dad said, "Don't be so hard on yourself. Be ambitious, but don't be unhappy."

I was ambitious and unhappy. That was the worst thing. I couldn't be like Shabaneh and say, "It doesn't matter whether you continue your studies or not. What's the big deal?" Or say, "You could just continue your studies here." Being content with the way things were made me throw up. It made me feel old. I always felt like I was one step behind myself. I had to run. I had to score a home run. I did. I was admitted. This is the last dream. When I get my doctorate, I'll be done. I'll go to work all day long. In the evening, I will just sit and watch a movie without worrying about anything. Once a week I will go to a salon. Every month I will travel. I think it was Kieślowski who, after finishing *Rouge*, had just let go, saying he wanted to go to a faraway place, sit in a villa on a couch, and keep smoking and drinking until he died. When I finish my PhD, I will be like him. How wonderful it would be to be so content with life, not to want to do anything other than having fun and then dying.

The door opens. Catherine Deneuve walks out. She seems agitated.

"Go in. I have to write my statement of purpose again. She said it has to be handwritten."

I go in. On the other side of the door, it's as if I've walked into a small house in another country. This is foreign land. Not only the people but also the design of the room is different. There's a living room set in the middle of the room. A few Black men and women sit on the sofa and are busy talking to a woman in French. I feel lost. No one is heeding me. I don't know who I should ask. A door opens, and a woman walks out of a room. I tell her, "*J'ai un appointment avec Mademoiselle Shabestari.*" I make sure to use Mademoiselle, not Madame, so as not to be rude. She says I need to wait there and then disappears. A voice behind me tells me to follow her.

I turn around. It's Shabestari. She has some papers in her hand. She doesn't look at me and just rushes into one of the rooms. I follow her. She sits down at her desk. I sit in the chair across from her. She reaches out her hand. I open my folder and give her my original documents. She browses through them. She immediately throws a few of them into the dustbin under her desk.

"The copies?"

I give her two sets of copies. She gives one back to me. She holds my statement of purpose in one hand and my résumé in the other and glances through them quickly.

"What have you been doing since you finished school?"

"I worked."

"Where?"

I want to tell her I tutored. I taught kids mathematics and physics. I want to tell her, "How do you think I made so much money? I worked my ass off to put this money together," but I just swallow my words. I've been told that any work unrelated to one's major would prompt negative points.

"In an engineering firm. My employer's letter is in there."

"This says nine months. Your graduation date is three years ago."

"I was studying French."

Her eyebrows lift as if she is saying, "I have nothing to do with this. It's you yourself who are fucking up your life." I wish that for a moment I could turn into Brad Pitt in *Fight Club* and bring down her face with my punches.

"Your financial documents?"

"They're in there."

"Just these?"

"Do you need something else?"

"Do you have anything else?"

I must not get upset. I'm at her mercy. I fidget in my seat. I take a deep breath in. "If there's anything else I need, please tell me. I can procure it," I say slowly, taking my time with my words.

"Your bank statement?"

"I don't have much in the bank. Should I bring it?"

"How should I know? It wouldn't hurt. You know better yourself. Documents for your residence there?"

"My dorm reservation receipts are in there."

"It needs to be finalized."

"You've accepted the same receipts before, from others. To make the reservation final, they ask for one year's rent in advance."

"That's none of my business. This is the law here. Press your fingers here."

She shows me a machine with a slot for four fingers. I press my fingers on it. It beeps.

"Your left hand too."

I press the fingers of my left hand.

"Put both your thumbs here, in the middle. Look here."

She raises her palm. When I look at it, she snaps a picture. I don't even get a chance to take off my glasses or run a hand through my hair. She gets up to leave. If she leaves, I don't have anyone to turn to anymore. I ask her, "When should I bring my supporting documents?"

"The sooner the better."

"Should I make an appointment?"

"You don't need an appointment. Put them in an envelope and hand it over at the door."

"This door? When will I hear back?"

"Not sure. It can be anywhere between three weeks to three months."

"I have to start classes in forty days."

She doesn't respond and walks out into the hallway. I follow her. The Black men and women are gone. She opens the door and calls out, "Number four."

The shy boy gets up. I walk out. Catherine Deneuve rushes toward her, waving a piece of paper in the air. "I wrote it," she tells Shabestari.

"Wait here. I'll call you."

Before Catherine Deneuve can say anything, Shabestari closes the door. The girl is confused. "What happened just now?"

"She's nuts, poor woman."

"Yes, they're all mad. What did she tell you?"

"Nothing. I need to provide more financial documents. I also have to finalize my dorm reservation. Do you know if I can do that without paying the whole year rent?"

"Don't worry about that. Listen to me. Find someone who lives where your school is. Tell them to write an affidavit that says they will host you and email it to you along with scans of their residence permit, lease, and utility bills."

"Will that do it?"

"Yes, that's what I did."

Who could I find in Toulouse on such short notice? I'll find someone. This isn't something to lose sleep over. Misagh had warned me that leaving would cost me a lot. When I was ready to mail my documents, I called Misagh, who had just left for Canada. "If you have it in you, get it rolling. If you are ready to pay the price. I gave away my whole life. I gave away Leyla," he had said.

"Was it worth it?"

He paused. Then he said he wasn't sure. I wish he had given me a straight answer. I wish he knew. That would make things easier. I shouldn't think about that now. It should've been worth it, because otherwise Misagh was not mad enough to continue to stay there. If he realized it was not worth it, he would definitely come back. Leyla is still waiting for him. I shouldn't give up. There is only one more thing left to do. This is not going to be easy. I'm going to live in another country. They say human beings can adapt to anything. They can dry out whole seas, move mountains, or, I don't know, tear down trees in a jungle. Providing documents for a place of residence would be nothing. I can call Samira. She probably knows someone in Toulouse. I check my watch. It's past one. I should go to work. I should show my face to Moghadam so that he won't bug Shabaneh about her friend not showing up to work. And then I should go to Sogol's house this evening. She has a math exam tomorrow. Or maybe I won't go. If I'm as tired as I am right now, I won't. But I can't. Her mother has called ten times. I need to repay my debt to Arsalan as soon as I can. Shabaneh might want to break up with him, but then feel obligated to stay with him because I owe him money.

I tell Sayeh, "I have to get to work. I'll see you later."

She asks for my phone number. I find the exit. It was so hard to come in that I don't really want to simply leave. I have thought so much about Misagh today that now I'm missing Leyla. She has to go to the newsroom this afternoon. I should call her. Maybe we can grab some lunch together and then we can head to work. I open the door. The world outside is the real world, full of the burning sun of the month of Mordad and the screaming sounds of private taxis.

Fall

ONE

I SPRAY THE CLEANER OVER the dried yellow stain of yogurt on the glass table. I straighten my back and wait for the blue drops of the cleaner to dissolve the yellow pieces of yogurt, and maybe from among them grass and gems will grow and turn the house into a garden full of flowers. I hold the phone to my ear and say, "And now I'm waiting for it to work. My back hurts from scrubbing this table. It doesn't get clean no matter what method I use."

"Why don't you use a scouring pad?"

"It might scratch the glass."

I continue to hold the phone with my shoulder and bend over the table. I rub the cloth over the stain. Instead of growing into a forest full of trees, the yellow pieces of yogurt turn into desert sand, dried and cracked, sticking to the cloth. A few stubborn pieces don't budge. I've reached rocks. I sit at the table and get at the rocks with my fingernail. "Did you have fun?" Mom asks.

"Yes, it was fun. I had been meaning to ask everyone to come over for a long time. I thought that now that Samira is in town and Roja hasn't left yet, it was as good a time as ever to bring everyone together. Where is Samira?"

"Their flight last night was delayed. They got here at three in the morning. She went to put Arian to bed, otherwise he would start whining."

I rub the cloth over the table once again. It's neither a forest nor a desert anymore. It's all clean, like a calm sea shining in the sunshine. Arian's Batman toy lies next to the table leg. It looks as if it has defeated all the bad guys and then, burned out after all this winning, fallen asleep right there. "Arian has become very naughty. He didn't stay put for one moment last night. He kept making a mess. He forgot his toy here," I said.

I grab a large green trash bag from the plastic bags drawer in the cabinet. Mom's voice, praising the wit and capabilities and beauties and who knows what else of her grandson nonstop, is drowned out by the rustling sound of the bags.

"I wish you could arrange to come to Ahwaz too, Leyla. We could all be together after a lifetime. You can bring Arian's toy with you."

"I can't, Mom. I have a lot of work. It's just the two of us at the culture desk. There would be no one to wrap up our page."

Plastic bag in hand, I start walking around the house to collect whatever trash is left. Empty bottles, fruit peels, cigarette butts, dirty napkins, and any remaining joyful detritus of last night's party. "There is no way this house is getting clean again. I've been scrubbing and cleaning since I woke up this morning," I say.

"That's what happens at parties. They turn your life upside down. You should've asked Ms. Molouk to come help you out."

"There were only eight of us, so I thought I wouldn't need her. Poor Shabaneh helped out. She came over the day before, and we cooked together. And yesterday, she took my keys and came over early, while I was still at work, so that the guests wouldn't have to wait outside." I leave the trash bag by the door so that I remember to take it out when I leave for work.

"She's such a sweet friend. But you didn't get home after your guests had arrived, did you?" Mom asks.

"No, I went in early and finished by early evening. I should get going, Mom. We have a lot of work at the newsroom on Saturdays. I should finish off things here at home and leave for work."

I hang up. It's not yet ten in the morning. I didn't get to sleep until the wee hours, but it was because I was excited about my page today. Like the old days when I could feel the beating of my heart in my temples and the bottom of my throat would start to taste sweet because I was going to see you during morning classes. It was still dark when I got up. While I was cleaning up the apartment, I drew ten different layouts of today's page on a piece of paper. I moved the pictures up and down and moved the boxes for each article around to make the special feature what it needed to be, the very feature for which I've been staying long hours at work for a week now, the very feature that Amir said only I could do well. He said, "Once a week we'll be running a dedicated cultural feature in your section. I believe you can do it. Think of some ideas and let's talk later. After we publish the first one, we'll get a better sense of what we want to do with it."

For the past week, I've been taking notes and crossing them out and holding meetings to make sure everything is in place. Now everything is ready for today. At noon, right before the layout room gets busy, like a mother preparing her daughter on her wedding day, I'll wrap up my special feature so that it can go to press at night, all beautiful and ready.

I only have an hour left and half the house is still a mess. I won't clean up completely now. I want the shine from last night's party to stay in my house. The candles Shabaneh lit around the apartment, the china set I brought out from the back of the chest after two years and is still on the drying rack, the large, dirty pots still on the stove, the overstuffed trash can and the knotted bags next to it that go all the way to the middle of the kitchen, the serving bowl full of chocolate, and the yellow stains on the table and the kitchen counter and the couch. When I get back from work tonight, tired and happy, I want to be reminded that my apartment was full of guests last night. Rahman had leaned his broom on the wall and asked me, "Do you need help?"

"Yes, please, Rahman. Take my keys. There are still two bags left in the trunk. Please bring those up. I have guests tonight."

When I told him I had guests, I felt something sweet at the bottom of my heart. I had repeated those words a hundred times since the morning. "Sir, please give me your best parsley. I have guests tonight." "I want your best oranges, good enough to be served to guests. Take out the smaller ones." "Add half a kilo of cake rolls as well. I'm afraid it won't be enough for my guests." I asked the shopboys to take the bags to my car and tipped all of them. I had been paid after two months of work. I had been paid and I was the lady of my own home. I was the lady of my home and I wanted to throw a party. Throwing a party is the peak of femininity. After all this time, I wanted my femininity back. I wanted to go shopping at a huge bazaar, a bazaar that smelled like fresh chicken and fish and herbs and fruits all mingled together; where thousands of tanned and scrawny shop-boys with bony, dirty hands would pick up fruit and look at me and flutter around me like butterflies and follow me and put my bags in my car. I wanted a ton of plastic bags piling up on the kitchen table. I wanted to have to check on three pots simultaneously. I wanted hot oil that splattered around and the sweetness of a burnt finger that would go in my mouth and be soothed. I wanted the sound of a knife chopping mushrooms over a wooden board while I broke out into an old song with the rhythm of the wooden board and the knife and the mushrooms. I wanted the water in the rice pot to boil over and ruin the stovetop and release the nice smell of the moist rice-cooking cloth. I wanted to run out of plates to serve the food and suddenly break a bowl but not have any tears fall over its breaking. All of this sounded like liberation, not worries.

I had shouted, "You don't want me to come, right? Yes, I know, you don't want me to come. You didn't even ask me once whether I wanted to come. You made up your mind all by yourself. And now you tell me I should go ahead and apply if I want to?"

You had sat down on the floor to gather the broken pieces of the bowl. You had said, "Calm down, Leyla. You know I can't live without you. Nothing has happened yet. There's still plenty of time to fill out an application."

I wished we had sat down together to collect the broken pieces, and that you had wiped away my tears with the tips of your fingers. I wanted to be hopeful and calm. I wanted to cook a delicious meal and invite a thousand people to our home so that I could forget about your announcement that you wanted to leave and my screaming and crying. I missed the times when people would praise my cooking. I missed that day a thousand years ago when, after the guests left, you took the dirty serving dish from me and put it on the counter and said, "You don't know how much I enjoy it when everyone praises your cooking, Leyli."

And I felt as if I had unburdened myself from the hardships of the world and lay on our red couch, happy and satisfied and tired. I wanted that same fatigue. After all this time. I didn't ask Rahman to bring the bags I already had in hand upstairs but carried them myself. I liked their weight in my hand. I brought them up the stairs and ran out of breath and put them down on the floor on each landing and took a happy breath in. The taut handles of the plastic bags left beautiful red marks on my fingers. I left everything I had bought on the kitchen table and lay on the couch to calm the burning feeling in my back, getting lost in thoughts about how to set the table and how to dress the salad, pushing all other thoughts out of my mind. I had found the good day that had kept escaping me and I was waiting for Shabaneh to come so we could start our work.

I let the living room stay messy and walk to my bedroom. I gather up my sheets and blanket and put them up on the bed. Since I started sleeping on the floor, I've stopped looking for you the moment I wake up. It's better for me this way. For both of us. I grab my light green Turkman manteau that I bought from Haft-e Tir and put it on. Everyone at work said it was pretty. The joyful green complements the red nail polish I put on last night. Roja said, "I can't believe we're getting to see you with nail polish before we die."

"Misagh didn't like nail polish."

"Yes, Misagh didn't like it, and you play the piano, so you can't grow your nails long. I know it all by heart. But when do you ever play the piano anymore, Leyla?"

"I want to start again. Believe me."

She took a slice of orange and put it in her mouth and withdrew into herself once again. What was wrong with her last night? She laughed and all, but, well, I know her better than that. She was not excited about Shabaneh's dishes and her eyes looked glazed and red. Shabaneh said Roja has not been feeling well for the past two days. She said, "She doesn't tell me anything. You ask her. She's been very sad. I feel sorry for her."

I tuck my headscarf behind my ear and start the car. The sooner I get to work, the better. I can finish early and then meet up with Roja. The traffic on the highway is heavy—like every other day. That's good. I can take my phone out of my purse and call Roja. She picks up after just two rings.

"Leyla! Were your ears ringing? Your party is continuing here. We were just talking about last night with Arsalan and Shabaneh."

I laugh. She doesn't. Her tone sounds bitter, even on the other side of the line. Very bitter. My smile disappears from my lips.

"Continuing?"

"Shabaneh brought the leftovers you gave her for lunch to share with me and Arsalan."

"She cooked them herself. Last night I started to like Arsalan for the first time. He seems like a good guy."

"Yes, I'd told you so."

Her voice is drowned out by the sound of a car horn. Perhaps she has walked to the office window again. She speaks in a low voice, "He's okay. I mean I hope he's okay. I think he could be good for Shabaneh. He's smart and knows how to manage life. He can pull Shabaneh out of her situation at home, with her mom, and Mahan. But he is also very stubborn, and Shabaneh doesn't know how to handle him well. I think she loves him, but I don't know why she keeps saying he's just a regular guy."

"That's actually a good thing. You know where you stand with him. He wouldn't just get up and go and leave Shabaneh behind."

"Right. This one is not going anywhere. Everyone's saying you should come have lunch with us. Come on. You still have time before work."

"No, I have to go in earlier today. I have a lot of work."

"You and your work!"

The words that come out of her mouth are definitely hers, but her voice, I can tell, is not. I know that something is squeezing her throat with long yellow claws and is closing down her vocal passages. I could tell since the night before last, when she brought me the grilled eggplants and took Shabaneh home. I ask her, "What's going on with you? Are you okay?"

"I'm not bad. How about yourself?"

As she herself says all the time, she's wearing iron armor and doesn't allow anyone in. "I'm good. I had lots of fun last night."

"I had fun too. It reminded me of the old times. When we were all doing fine."

The long yellow claws squeeze my throat too now.

"Are you free this evening? If I finish early, maybe we could do something together."

She inhales so deeply and with so much noise that I can hear the air circling in her lungs.

"Not sure. Maybe," she says, in such a way that her sad breath blows all the way through her phone and rattles in my ear. The claws squeeze my insides. Sad sighs don't suit her. When was the last time she felt sad? I can't remember. The weight of her sigh sits on my heart. Sighs are contagious, like yawns. They spread through the air and crash down on the hearts of people like me who have sorrow receptors. I receive Roja's sorrow through the phone. When I hang up, a strong, sad, poisonous breath leaves my mouth through my teeth and fills the air inside my car with envy for a thousand things that should be but are not.

I roll down the window and exchange the poisonous sigh with the cool breeze of fall. You had turned the car air conditioner on and I was thrilled by the cool breeze brushing against my face. You said, "Leyli, Leyli, I want to spend all summer under your fall-colored hair."

You said, "Your hair is this color so that I can be reminded of the fall in the middle of the heat of summer."

I turn onto the street where the office is, where all the leaves have turned golden. Today all the traffic lights on my way were red. What if that's a sign of a bad day? If I find a parking spot on this very street, that means it's going to be a good day, I decide. My heart is pounding as I drive slowly down the street. I seek the good vibes of today among these cars. But there is no spot. I exhale and turn to the next street. Right behind me a car leaves its spot. I knew this was going to be a good day. Of course it's going to be a good day. I'm going to put together my own page. I put the shift in reverse and parallel park my car.

I say a loud hello to the guard at the door and I remember to ask how his sick wife is doing before I head up the stairs. I'm early. No one seems to be here yet; the building feels empty. Now, like an overeager passenger who got to the station too early, I should just sit calmly in my seat and wait for other passengers before we can all get going and start our day. Amir, however, is already here. It's strange for him to have come in so early. He is wearing his usual white shirt and sits at the society desk and drinks tea with another early riser from that group. When he looks up, I get nervous. Whenever I see him, even the most basic things seem hard, even impossible. I forget how to say hi and how to sit down and a hundred other things. I say hi before putting down my purse and laptop. He smiles and says, "Go pour yourself a glass of tea and come have some breakfast with us."

I thank him and say I've already had breakfast. He gets up and walks toward my desk.

"You're in early."

"I had guests last night. I got up early."

"Everyone gets up late when they have guests. How come you're the exact opposite?"

He laughs and runs his hand through his beard. I laugh but don't admit that I couldn't sleep because I was so excited about the upcoming special feature. He says, "It shows that you didn't sleep. Your eyes are red."

He sits down in my chair. The weight of my stuff has been hurting my shoulder, so I lay it all down on the desk. I stand in front of him and, like a child who is answering questions from her favorite teacher, I recite every little detail of the page to him from memory. I tell him I had already gathered all the pictures and approved all the articles by yesterday afternoon. Then, waving my hands in the air, I give him a presentation of the complete layout, how each piece and image on the page looks and where it's placed. He rests his chin in his hand and looks at me with a peaceful smile. He murmurs a "That's all wonderful" and gets up. He says, "It's still early to finalize the layout. I'm headed to the daily meeting. Do your own work until it's time; then I'll call you."

I follow him with my eyes. He turns around and puts his hands on my desk and says in a low voice, "You see? I told you you could. I've always had faith in you."

He has faith in me. As he leaves the newsroom, his sentence

repeats in my mind a dozen times and brings all the blood in my body to my face. The heat of my breath warms up my lips, and once again I hear, "I've always had faith in you."

I wish you were here and could see how they count on me and they have faith in me at the job you always told me was not for me. You had pushed your plate away and thrown your spoon on it. The red sauce from the chicken splashed all over your yellow T-shirt. With a voice that didn't belong to you, you shouted, "For a whole week now I've been begging you, since you haven't applied for school, to at least go ahead and send in your documents to apply for an F-2 visa so that you can come as my wife. Then you sit here in front of me and tell me you found a job at a magazine? You—you want to drive me crazy. Is that even a job for you? Two months from now, when you get tired of it all, it will be too late."

"I won't get tired of it," I said under my breath.

You stood up and knocked your chair over. The sound of the chair hitting the floor behind you startled me. I looked at you. Your face was completely red, the same color as the sauce splashed on your T-shirt. Your voice rose even higher.

"You've tried out dozens of jobs in the past two years and you've grown tired of all of them. When are you going to grow up? I'm tired of your immaturity. My life is not like your Dad's, where everything is handed to you for you to do whatever you like and not even break a sweat. I want to live like an adult. You won't let me. I'll leave, Leyla. I'll get a divorce and leave. I swear to God I'm going to leave. And you'll regret it."

I served myself some salad and said in a calm voice, "Even mentioning divorce is bad. If everything goes through and you leave, if everything is fine there and you stay, then you can bring it up."

I put my spoon and fork on my plate, lowered my eyes, and added, "You can't go. You won't leave without me."

You took the car keys and left the house in the same T-shirt. I thought I should have at least shaken some salt over the stain so that when you got back it would come out more easily. The sound of the door slamming behind you startled me once again. I shouldn't have said that last sentence. I shouldn't have provoked you by being obstinate. If I hadn't started this stupid competition, you wouldn't have left without me. You weren't my enemy. Why was I fighting you? If I had talked about it calmly, saying, "Let's not leave," if I had sat down and talked to you and told you, "I can't live without you," you wouldn't have left without me.

Roja kept saying, "Stop being so hard on yourself. He had made up his mind. No matter what you did, he would have left anyway. You went down separate paths."

We went down separate paths? Since when? How? I can't remember. Maybe from that day you sat across from me and told me you had given it some thought and you wanted to get a PhD and become a professor. You said the way to do it would be for you to leave, and I, instead of acting like we were one unit with one shared life, instead of telling you that whatever decisions you made, I would stand by your side, I separated myself from you and told you to do whatever you wanted and that I would not stop you.

My phone keeps ringing. It's Mom.

"Leyla darling, Dad was saying that he would love it if you and Samira could both be here with us after so long. That would make the poor man so happy. When you get to work, ask if you can have someone cover for you so you can come to Ahwaz."

"I'm already at work, Mom. I'll ask and see, but I don't think so. I have a lot of work."

I don't tell her that I'm in no mood to be at home and that I hate all the parties she'll be throwing for Samira's visit home. Dr. X who is head of that hospital and Professor Y from that university and the rest of the gang, with their wives, filling up the whole house like gas molecules in an enclosed space. The wives who all look like twins, because they all go to the same hair salon, the hair salon lucky enough to be name-dropped by all the doctors' wives in Ahwaz that year. One day they all have blond hair with golden lipstick, the next they all have black hair with red lipstick. They all talk nonstop, and in the middle of their chatter about their latest trips to this or that island and checking up on the news of their kids who study medicine in Hungary and Canada and Malaysia and I-don't-know-where-else, little by little they tentatively move the conversation to me and, in the end, they ask me timidly about you in a low voice. One by one, like ants moving in to eat a dead cockroach, they gather around the corpse of your memories. They argue with one another and begin to disagree. One says I made a mistake by not going with you, because one should stay by one's husband's side. Another runs a kind hand over my head and says, "You were too good for him, my dear Leyla. Your husband was not a family man." Another says all men are like this: ungrateful. There's also an old woman who, every time, says, "A woman should be diplomatic, my dear. Diplomacy. You were not diplomatic enough." And I do not like to have to explain to someone that, in their own home, even famous female politicians who run the world cannot rely on anything other than their womanhood to keep their husbands' hearts close.

You had lost your heart; you didn't want to stay anymore. No one could have kept you, least of all me; I had always held my hands loose around your body, encouraged you to fly myself. And like a bird in the sky, you flew up and went farther and farther until I could not see you anymore. And now, no matter how hard I stare at that blue patch of sky where you disappeared and shout out that I still have not sung all my love songs to you, you will not come back to me. I don't say any of this to the women. Instead, with a smile on my face, little by little, seat by seat, I move away from their group and reach the kitchen. Like the last soldier standing in an occupied town, I take refuge by the cold walls of the kitchen. I swallow my Librium pill with a glass of cold water and I can't tell whether it's the cold water making me calm or the pill has had such a quick effect. They continue to talk about me even without me until dinnertime. After dinner, it's someone else's turn.

I check the time. It's still early for work. I still have enough time to go through today's paper from beginning to end. I walk to the kitchen and pour myself a dark tea. I inhale the steam and then leave my glass on the table for it to take its time cooling down. I sink into my chair and grab the paper. I arrange the middle pages by heart where they belong and begin to leaf through it as if I'm an old man sitting at the park with all the time in the world to look through the paper. He gets to my page, and his eyes remain locked on it. I feel a flutter in the pit of my stomach. I take another look to make sure everything is in order. It is. Amir has put my name on top of one of the pieces. I read through it quickly. The editors have once again changed a comma to a dash. I should remind them again how much I hate dashes. But it doesn't really matter. The old man is drawn into the piece and is not bothered at all by the dash. When he gets to the end of the piece, he looks back at the author's name. My heart begins pounding faster. The old man slowly shakes his head, murmurs an elongated "Wow," and remembers to tell his friend or wife or son about this piece before moving on to the next article.

I love my page so much. It's my little baby. A baby that is birthed anew and needs me to sew him new clothes every day. I can sit him down on my lap and look him up and down. Then get pregnant and give birth to him all over again and watch how he grows up in one day and follows the other kids to his independent life, separate from me.

I was sitting in the waiting room, and the receipt I held was wet with my sweat. I was surrounded by people who had bottled something from their bodies and had brought it with them—blood and urine and tumors, good or bad. I had collected myself and was taking care of the new part of me. Every time the loudspeaker crackled, I heard my own name and jumped from my seat. I was terrified. I didn't want them to hand me a fucking piece of paper and tell me he didn't exist. My purse was on my belly, and I had wrapped my arms around him. I knew I wasn't alone. I could feel him. He was sleeping peacefully at the bottom of my belly. He and I had become friends over the past few days. It seemed as if he had always been there, but I hadn't seen him. We talked with each other. I mean I talked, and he passed his words to me in my head in a way I could understand. We had gone to Bahar Street and he had told me what he liked. He liked the blue clothes. I imagined he was a boy. I bought him a sweater and a hat. Both blue. When Roja saw the clothes, she said, "Are you insane? It's been four months since Misagh left."

"I've been nauseous for three days. They say mothers can feel such things. And I have a feeling."

"Let's go to the lab so they can do the blood work to be sure."

"I don't want to."

"You don't want to because you know there is nothing there. Don't turn this into a thing, Leyla. You'll get hurt."

Shabaneh asked, "But what if she really is pregnant? I'll raise him myself, Leyla. I hope he looks like Arian, chubby and light-skinned, with light hair."

Then she turned to Roja.

"Do you think Misagh is going to come back if she's pregnant?"

Roja stood up.

"You both are crazy, and you're driving me crazy too."

You *would* come back. I knew you would. There was no way you would leave me all alone with this child. You were never someone who abandoned people. You had left just to frighten me. But I didn't understand why it was taking you so long to come back. That day, though, it didn't really matter that you weren't there. Even if you were never coming back, I was not alone anymore. He was sleeping peacefully in my belly and I had to take care of him. I walked with care to make sure he and I and us weren't disturbed. I didn't want to take a test. There was no need for one. The court, though, would need to see the results of a pregnancy test and make sure they were negative before they signed off on the divorce. I knew I was pregnant the moment they said I needed to get the test. And there I was, sitting, alone and ragged and beaten, waiting for my turn. When they called me, I walked to the reception, my knees trembling, struggling to hold my body upright. I handed the woman my crumpled receipt. "Are you okay? You look very pale," she said.

I muttered an "I don't know" through the lump pressing on my throat, the lump that had been lingering there since you left and that I couldn't swallow with anything, neither with water nor with bread, not even with the antibiotics I had to take for months. The lump didn't budge. The receptionist searched for my results for what felt like a lifetime. She glanced first at the paper and then at me and said, "It's negative."

Suddenly I felt emptied out. All the air in the waiting room drained out, and my loneliness clawed at me once again. For the past four months, the weight of the empty apartment had chewed on my flesh, leaving almost nothing, and now, the weight of my empty body was starting to chew on the final remainders of me from inside. He had died, and my hope that you would come back, that I would not be alone, raising a son whose name was Siavash or Farhad, who would grow up to become a pianist or a writer and who would never leave a girl behind all by herself, had died along with him. Something was pulling my heart out from my chest, shredding it and throwing it away. My knees could not hold my body up anymore. Suddenly everything disappeared from in front of my eyes. The chairs, the people, the reception desk. The sounds grew weaker and weaker, and a whiteness covered everything around me. When I opened my eyes, my face was wet, and the receptionist was saying, "What happened? You poor thing, did you want a baby?"

Amir asks, "Have you seen my cell phone, Leyla?"

He scatters all the papers in his letter tray and searches through them. He opens his leather briefcase and closes it. He is worried, and on his face, there are no longer the signs of infinite calmness usually hidden in his beard but revealing themselves as necessary. His being worried makes me nervous. I ask him, "What's wrong?"

"I can't find my phone."

I get up, pick up the papers, and pile them together on one side of the desk. His cell phone is under one of them.

"Thanks, Leyla."

"You're making me worried. Is something the matter?"

"No, don't worry."

"Are my pages laid out? Do you have any updates?"

After two months working with him, I'm still not sure how I should address him, formally or more casually. Recently, I've been using more of a casual tone, but I can't yet call him by his first name. I still address him by saying "look," or "excuse me," or whatever else saves me from calling him Amir or Mr. Salehi. He says, "Not yet. Don't be in such a rush."

He walks away, but his concern lingers in the air. Like the magic of the old fairy godmother in *Cinderella*, it swirls around me and dresses my happy body in a different outfit. My heart begins to pound in my throat, and a bitter taste fills my mouth. It's the fall depression, I know it. Depression can come in the spring, or in the fall; it can be primary or secondary; whenever it wishes, it can enter under a new name and make my throat bitter. I mustn't think about it. Dad said, "Distract yourself, my darling. Think of good things, like your job. Think about how much you love it."

I think about the special features I will be putting together, about the rosy days of the future that will all pass by with the excitement of Mondays when my new special features page is published. I imagine myself staying late at the newsroom and working. I see people crowding around newsstands in the streets on Mondays, leafing through the paper and looking over one another's shoulders to see my feature. The headlines of the articles find their way to the front page, the paper gets sold out in every newsstand by noon, every website shares my pieces, and those who have been exposed by the article call the paper every day and Amir defends me and answers all their allegations.

"Hi, Leyla, you're here early."

Saghar drops her stuff on her desk and sits down.

"Your hands look so nice with nail polish! How was your party?"

"It was great. I wish you had come too."

"Sorry I couldn't make it. Is anyone here? Ehsan? Amir?"

"Amir is here. Ehsan isn't."

"What are we working on today?"

"I haven't checked the news yet. It's still early."

Saghar puts her headphones on and disappears behind her monitor. I look around the newsroom as it gradually fills up, like it does every day. I love these people. I feel happy when we work together and we laugh together. This is my safe space. My peaceful corner of the world. I can find refuge among my colleagues, and no one can hurt me here. I look at them and take a deep breath, feeling a happiness I'm just beginning to find underneath the shards of my heart.

I open different news sites to see what's going on today. The headlines parade in front of my eyes, and going through them I see the image of the page I'm putting together. I draw the layout on a piece of paper for the thousandth time. I have to leave today's work for later, after I'm done with the layout. It won't be too late. I can postpone meeting with Roja for another time. I can even tell her to come to my place later tonight and just stay over. I probably won't be able to sleep tonight either. Like two months ago, when I was waiting for the first issue of the paper and I spent all night long tossing and turning in sheets wet with my sweat. At four in the morning, I got into my car and drove to the closest newsstand. It was closed. I opened my car window. I drove around and let the cool end-of-summer early-morning breeze brush against my face. Around six I went back to the newsstand and waited until it opened up so I could buy a copy of the paper. A new edition, issue number one. I lingered around for an hour and watched people who walked by the newsstand and picked up the paper. Then I went and bought a big chocolate cake and went to Roja and Shabaneh's office. Roja said, "If you're in a good mood like this every day, cake will be on *me* every day." I uploaded the page on my blog and waited for you to see it.

I open my blog page again now. There's no sign of you today either. I'm sure you read my posts. How could you not? It's your pride that stops you from commenting. I've been blogging about my new job for two months, and you haven't yet commented. I've written about all the rosy days of the past two months. The first day the paper was published, the day Amir had me write the front-page story. The day the headline for the news piece I wrote was put on the front page and the editor in chief praised my work in front of everyone.

I had yelled, "But once upon a time you used to love my recklessness."

"Recklessness is for fun, for college days. It's not for your whole life. Grow up, Leyla, please."

You had stopped calling me Leyli. For a long while now you were calling me just Leyla. You didn't love me anymore, and I had become Leyla, the way I was for everyone else. I had thrown the magazine on the table.

"I won't grow up. I'm going to stay here and do the work that I love to do."

I check the time. I feel a hot liquid pouring over my heart. It's getting late. I wave my hand in front of Saghar's face, so she takes her headphones out of her ears.

"Do you know where Amir went? He was supposed to call me so we could do the final layout of the page."

"I don't know. Go see if the articles are ready. Maybe the typesetters aren't done yet."

She puts her headphones back in and begins tapping on the stone floor with her feet. I look at the desk next to us. The editor of the society page isn't there. Neither is the editor of the sports page. I look at the monitors. Everyone is just killing time on the internet. I get up and walk out of the newsroom. Even the old censor guy who always sits in the office across from us isn't here. I walk downstairs. The typesetters are busy typing fast, and the sound of their long nails on the keyboards reminds one of the sewing machines of a dressmaking workshop.

"Excuse me, I was wondering if the pieces I sent you on Wednesday are ready to go. Can I see them?"

The head of typesetting shows me the letter tray.

"Just make sure you don't make a mess."

I look through the prints. All the articles I've approved are there. I pick them up and walk upstairs to tell Amir that everything is ready. We should begin the layout soon so that if there are any problems I have enough time to make the necessary edits carefully. It's getting late. Saghar takes out her headphones.

"Did you find Amir?"

"No, but all the pieces are ready. I'll call him now."

"He should come over to check the new sections as well. It's already late."

I dial his number. With every unanswered ring, my heart pounds even harder in my chest.

"He's not answering."

"Maybe he's still in a meeting. Let's carry on with the other work. He'll show up eventually."

I sit down and drink a sip of my cold tea. I open my email. "Read and forward," "Men's parenting," "Once-in-a-Lifetime prices," "Thanks for last night." The last one is from Shabaneh. She writes that she and Mahan had a lot of fun last night. She writes, "Colorful clothes suit you so much. You should always wear colors . . . Mahan couldn't sleep all night long after the party and he made you a drawing. I scanned it so you could see it today. I'll give you the original when we meet next." I open the attachment. There's a window with eight adults and one child standing under it. All of them have circles for bodies, and their arms and legs are straight lines. He's colored in only one of the figures. It has light brown hair and wears a dress patterned in yellow, red, green, and blue. That's me. Next to me, he drew himself. He's taller than everyone else, and over his head he wrote a large *M* so that I can recognize him. I wish Mahan were mine.

I open my chat list at the corner of the screen and search for Shabaneh. Her light is on. I type, "How are you?"

"Doing okay. How about you? Did you finalize the layout?"

"Not yet. Amir was supposed to let me know. He's late. I'm getting worried."

"You always worry about everything. Stop!"

She adds a smiley face. I do too. I write, "Any news of Roja? Is she feeling better?"

"She seems better today, but she still seems distracted."

"I'll talk to her tonight. She's probably worried about leaving. The closer it gets, the harder it is for her. Misagh was like that too. The last few days, he was constantly in a daze."

She doesn't type a response. That's good. I don't want to talk about you. Not today. That's the good thing about chatting. Whenever you want, you say something, and when you don't, you just don't type anything and disappear without even saying goodbye. You can laugh without anyone realizing you're crying. You can simply ignore something you don't like, rest your chin in your hands, stare at the monitor, and pretend that you're busy. You can be sitting at your computer but choose the offline option. In the blink of an eye, your name disappears from the list, and no one gets concerned. She writes, "Sorry, Arsalan called me over."

"How is he?"

"He's doing okay. He's very funny today. Since the party, he's been acting like a husband. He's been so nice!"

She laughs at the end of her sentence, adding a little devil emoji with white teeth. I send a laughing emoji with its mouth open and its jaws move up and down. We've become yellow circles and we both know that we are staring at our monitors, our faces more somber than ever.

I was sitting on the couch, staring at the monitor. It had been a long time since you closed the door behind you and left for the airport. It had become dark and then light, and I had not touched the lights. Knots had formed in my heart and then become untied, and an unpleasant taste filled my throat. I felt hot, then my body was covered in cold sweat, and then I felt hot again. My bones felt dry—they hurt. The pain swirled in my arms and moved to my legs and then it started all over again. You were my opium, and I was in withdrawal. Thoughts circled in my mind, making a thousand turns an hour, and the acrid taste of them emptied into my stomach, making me sick. I wanted to throw up my brain and be done—empty. I was afraid to move. I was afraid to move and realize that I was awake and everything I had seen was real. I had slept on the couch and time and again I was jolted awake by the nightmare of your plane taking off. In one nightmare, my body was the runway, and your plane ripped it apart as it took off. In another nightmare, your plane turned into a missile that launched from our apartment, and its sound and fire made the walls collapse over my chest, suffocating me. I was afraid to fall asleep. I was afraid to look into our bedroom and see your clothes still on the bed. I was afraid to take a shower and wash your scent off my body. I was afraid to open the windows and let your breaths leave the house. All wet, my clothes clung to my body. There was no oxygen in the apartment. There was no height to the ceiling. I was jolted awake by the sound of the phone ringing a dozen times, but I didn't answer any of the calls. Roja came. She banged on the door, begged me, howled at me, but I did not open the door. I couldn't move my knees. I had no voice. I couldn't tell anyone that you had left. If my tongue turned in my mouth and my voice left the insides of my body and I told others that you had gone, your departure would turn into reality. I wished you were dead and not gone. If you were dead, all your good traits would stay with me and they would be enough for the rest of my life. But you had left me, and nothing good remained. I kept staring at the monitor and at your light, which was off. It was off and while it didn't turn on, you were still not gone, you had not arrived anywhere. You were waiting behind the door. You only had to knock and come in. You didn't. I got up and opened the door. You were not there. I came back to the couch. Your light was on, and before I could ask you where you were, you wrote,"I've arrived, Leyla. Everything is set. School, the apartment, everything. I wish you had come with me."

"How will you get through the summer without my hair?" I wrote back.

You didn't respond. You got through your summer. I didn't learn how. I was shown your pictures. Happy pictures of you in shorts, colorful yellow and green and red shirts that you never liked, and a cap that hid the waves of your hair, next to this bridge and that river, pictures in which you laughed. You laughed, but happy . . . I knew you were not. I could tell from your eyes.

"By the way, Leyla, I got you the piano teacher's number," Saghar says. She gets up, raising her interlaced fingers over her head, stretching, yawning.

"Thanks. Why isn't Amir coming, Saghar? I can't wait anymore," I say.

"I think you should go ahead and put your page together. Amir is so absentminded."

Amir is not absentminded. Why hasn't he come? Doesn't he know that I am waiting? Waiting as if I am about to get an award in front of everyone at school during the morning lineup, and before the bell rings, I keep running around the stronghold made of rocks in the school courtyard. We are holding each other's hands, turning in a circle, singing, "We've lost our handkerchief under the cherry tree." Losing. Being lost. Why are we taught, since childhood, about *losing* before we are taught anything about *finding*? It is perhaps because of these lessons that we end up losing things every day, piece by piece, things that we can never get ahold of again. We lose them, and our lives become emptier and emptier until nothing remains except a handful of dusty memories of what has been lost. I have to put my page together. I have to do something, whatever it is. When I do something, I get distracted. I can hide in a circular glass room and forget that I am alive. Then my heart calms down and stops beating so loud in my chest. I grab the articles, baffled soldiers in the hands of a defeated general, and walk upstairs. No one is in the stairwell. It's as if I came to work on a weekend. The halls are empty. The atmosphere is stale, and the clock, yawning, elongates time. Nothing looks like a Saturday noon at work, busy and filled with news. The layout assistants sit around the room, their backs to one another and staring at their monitors, with nothing to do. None of the staff writers are upstairs.

"The special feature on culture is ready. Can I begin putting my page together? I've already uploaded the pictures in the system," I ask the head layout assistant.

"Where is Mr. Salehi?"

"He isn't here yet, but I need to put the page together today. He insisted."

"You have to wait a bit. We're not sure what's going to happen."

"What's going to happen? We complete the page layout, and if there any edits, we will be told."

My cell phone rings. It's Saghar.

"Leyla dear, will you come downstairs? Amir is here."

My heart beats hard and feels drained. I put my soldiers under my arm, and we file back downstairs together. Like water flowing over the stairs. The hallway is crowded. People have gathered around in groups and are talking. It looks like the hallways in the family court building. I hear:

"It's temporary. It's going to be resolved."

"All bans are temporary, but we know this is the end."

It was six months after you had left. We were supposed to get divorced by consent. In room 311, I had an appointment with Judge Abbasi. A heavy file in my hands, I felt like I was walking on a void. I *am* walking on a void. I stop and take a breath. I force everything out of my mind. This is not real. Nothing is real.

"Can they defy the closing?"

"It's not clear what is going on."

"Defy what? Protest whom?"

I walk to our office. Amir is standing by our desk, and Saghar is standing in front of him. "Call Ehsan and the others. Tell them not to come in if they haven't left home yet. This place is just going to make them sad," he says in a low, hoarse voice.

I don't come forward. I didn't come forward. By the door, I saw an old judge, wearing a dark blue coat in the heat of the summer, sitting behind a desk covered with poisoned files, rummaging through documents. Amir turns around and sees me.

"There you are, Leyla dear. I'm sorry. I was in a meeting when you called. We have a problem and we don't know when it's going to be resolved."

He sounds calm and kind. Calm and sad. His face is downcast. He has aged. His eyes are small and bloodshot. Saghar sits down. I cannot bring myself to ask anything. I should not ask anything. If Amir says something, everything will become real. I should tell him not to speak. Not to speak at all, not to say a word. I cannot. My lips are locked. My lips were locked. I stood by the door and I could not move. The judge looked up.

"Can I help you, my girl?"

Amir takes a step forward and speaks. I wish he wouldn't.

"The paper is going to be shut down for a week. We still haven't been charged with anything, but they've ordered us to cease publication. Since we never received a formal warning, we hope it gets resolved soon. But . . . sit down, Leyla."

I sit down. My skin has turned into a hard shell through which nothing can pass. Like Niobe, I have turned into a rock, but unlike her, I am unable to shed tears.

"Don't worry. This isn't the first time. We already have a permit for another paper and we'll start over together in a few weeks. This time you'll be with us from the very beginning."

He puts his hand on my shoulder. He forces an ugly, bitter smile onto his lips. Someone calls him. His smile disappears. He leaves. The judge looked at me. I opened the folder and showed him my documents.

"I have power of attorney for my husband. For . . ." The word *divorce* didn't come loose in my mouth. My voice came out like a bullet you had placed in my throat. A camera flashes in my face. Someone has taken a picture. He lowers the camera and explains, "The news of the shutdown is going on the cover page. They need pictures."

Saghar puts her headphones down on her desk and looks at the others. One holds her head in her hands. Another leans on the wall. Someone else talks on his cell phone.

"No. Apparently the supervisory board had a meeting at noon. They just announced it . . . Our people went to a meeting to resolve the issue . . . No, they couldn't. They couldn't convince them."

My soldiers are damp in my hands. I put them on my desk and get up. I walk out of the office. A man sits on the stairs, his head between his hands. His shoulders tremble. The photographer takes a picture of him. The three typesetters walk out through the glass door, their purses on their shoulders. A young man storms out of the content supervision room, where the censor sits, and goes downstairs.

"It's a divorce by consent? Are you sure you don't want to think about it?" the judge asked.

"Are you okay, dear girl? Do you want to leave and come back a month from now?" the judge asked.

"Leyla, are you here?" Saghar is looking for me.

"Are you staying?"

"Should we stay?" I don't recognize my voice.

"I called everyone and told them not to come to work. Amir said we should leave but come back tomorrow morning. He said we should check in on the situation, as we wait for things to be resolved," she says.

"We are not children. And this is not the first time. We all know that we're not coming back to the paper tomorrow, or ever," she says.

The wedding officiant had pushed the book in front of me. "Sign here, my dear."

"Where?"

He put his finger on the page. I couldn't see the lines. I signed.

Auntie began celebrating. She threw a handful of noghl sweets on the book. They bounced up and down. You laughed.

"Bye."

I made my way through the court hallways and walked out like a sleepwalker. You were very far away that day. You were not breathing in this world. The man I divorced was not you. He was a dead man. I took a taxi and went to the airport. I don't remember buying a ticket, boarding a plane, and arriving home. I only remember the warmth of Dad's body as he held me tight in his arms.

"Why didn't you tell us, darling girl?"

I throw my purse over my shoulder and walk out the office building. I want Dad's warmth. I miss the days when he came back from his office, sat me and Samira across from him, drank his tea, and asked us, "Well, my girls, how is life going? Is it going well?"

I have to go to the airport. I will stay with Mom and Dad until the next newspaper gets rolling.

TWO

LIKE EVERY OTHER THURSDAY, IT'S noon when I get home. I haven't yet changed out of my work clothes when Mahan opens the door to our room and says, "Shaba, hurry up! Mom!"

I put my purse down on my desk and walk out of the bedroom still in my manteau. Mahan follows me. Mom walks out of the kitchen holding the phone to her ear. She extends her hand toward me and gestures to ask, "What should I do?" Startled, I stare at her. She silently mouths the words "Arsalan's mom."

"Why is she calling now?" I ask.

She throws her hand up in the air. This means she has cursed me a dozen times and wants me to shut up because I've caused her to lose face, because I don't understand anything, because she is miserable that one of her children is me, ignorant and stupid, and the other, Mahan. I lean toward her and whisper, "Please, Mom, tell her to call tomorrow. She had said she would call tomorrow. Please."

She turns around and goes back to the kitchen. I hear her say, "I'm sorry, ma'am, Shabaneh's father is not yet home. I'll call you myself later. Yes, I know how well acquainted the two of them are with one another, but without her father's permission . . ."

Mahan pulls my arm and we go to our room. I take my manteau off and sit at the edge of my bed. Mahan closes the door and sits down next to me. "Don't worry. Mom is not mad. She is just very tired," I reassure him.

He doesn't believe me. He too can guess that when Mom hangs up, she is going to scream at us for half an hour or so. Then she will hold her head in her hands and weep on and on and curse us and herself and life in general. That's why we are in our bedroom. We are hiding because we don't want to be exposed to her fury. We were hiding. I had sent Mahan behind the desk, the desk that has been sitting at this very corner of our room since our childhood. I had pulled all the sheets we had over Mahan's bed and straightened the bedding on top. If Mom found out that Mahan had once again wet his bed, she would kill him. She had said so herself. She had held Mahan's chin in her hand, brought his face close to hers, and said, "I'll kill you. Next time, I'll kill you." I had been standing behind him and felt my stomach churning when I had seen Mom's face. When I finished making the bed, I told Mahan to come out. I arranged his toy cars in front of him, and we played until Mom got back around noon. We played all the games he enjoyed. I thought he was going to be killed that afternoon and I wanted to keep him happy until then. When I heard the front door opening, I held Mahan in my arms, and we sat against the closet door. Mom opened the door to our room and shouted, "Where is this pee smell coming from again?"

No matter how long we wait, Mom doesn't open the door to our room. I can hear the angry thud of her footsteps around the apartment. Then comes the sound of her medication bag, the terrifying sound of plastic rustling, followed by ice from the icemaker dropping in a glass. I can hear in my mind the sound of her swallowing the pills next, and my stomach churns. I've memorized her smallest moves. I've heard all these consecutive sounds for a thousand years, and every time, without really knowing what I've been afraid of, my stomach has churned.

Like all the previous thousand times, nothing bad will happen this time either. It will all pass, except for my fear of the sound of her footsteps and the rustling of the plastic bag. Like every other time, Mahan gets as close to me as possible and throws his hands around me. Fuck me. Even my marriage causes this kid to suffer. I say, "Don't worry. Nothing's the matter."

Mom begins to sob loudly. She keeps saying, "Oh my God, Oh my God," and cries. There's really no reason for her to cry. I have nothing to do with this. She wreaks havoc over everything, regardless of whether it's big or small. I want to ignore her and let her cry as much as she wants, but Mahan's hiccupy breaths and his silent crying, as usual, without shedding tears, slap me in the face and squeeze every corner of my heart. I feel for Mahan. I feel for Mom. More than anyone I feel for myself. I loosen Mahan's arms from around me and walk out of the room. Mom sits on the couch and cries. I want to shout at her and tell her to stop. Tell her that she's ruined our whole lives, and I'm sick and tired of her. But another Shabaneh opens her mouth calmly and says, "What's going on, Mom? Why are you acting like this?"

She doesn't respond. Mahan stands by the door, his shoulders trembling. I take the glass of water from Mom's hand and bring it to her lips. "Drink this, Mom. Why are you crying? Did she say something to you? Did you take your pills?"

She pushes the glass away, and sobbing and gasping for breath, she says, "You made me lose face in front of his mother. She said the two of you have been going out for a year. How come she knows everything, but I don't?"

"She just meant we've been colleagues for the past year."

"If she meant colleagues, she would say colleagues. You don't need to make excuses. Do you think I'm stupid? You always act like I'm dumb. Everyone thinks I'm dumb."

She cries even harder. I swallow the lump in my throat and go back to our room. Mahan is still crying silently without shedding a tear. I look at him. He's grown so tall I only reach his shoulder. Tall men should not cry. They should never cry, even if they're 'mentally challenged' or whatever the fuck else you want to call it. When tall men cry, the world becomes shaky. It only hangs on by a thread, and can crumble down with the touch of a finger. I put my hand on Mahan's high shoulder and sit him down on the bed. I comb his disheveled hair with my fingers and say calmly, "Don't cry. I'm going to fix everything. When you come out of the bedroom in five minutes, she's going to be smiling."

He is not as naive as when he was a child. He has not bought into my words. I can tell from his breathing, which has not gone back to normal yet, and from his head, which he has not yet lifted up. As a last attempt, I ask him, "Do you want to talk to Leyla?"

He looks at me and nods yes. I call her and give him my cell phone before closing the door and walking to the living room. Mom is wiping away her tears. "What is this joke you're playing on us?

Why can't we have some happiness in this goddamn life? Why don't you give them a straightforward answer?"

I look down. I'm afraid to answer. I'm afraid that I'd open my mouth and say, "If I say yes, then Arsalan will come and we'll get married, and from the very next day, his mother will turn into a monster and come stay with us, wearing a black cloak and holding a hook, and never leave again. And he himself would beat me every day and not let me see Mahan ever again. Then you'll throw Mahan out into the street, and I won't be here to help him, and he'll wander around and weep in the streets and turn into a beggar and end up dying of hunger and cold in his ragged clothes at a street corner." I wish Dad hadn't said I should decide for myself. I wish Leyla, Roja, or even Mahan would say something. I don't know how to make a decision on my own. I wish it were already ten days, or ten months, or ten years from now. Then these hard days would already be over, and everything would have figured itself out. I tell her, "You need to have my back, Mom. You need to help me. If you get upset like this, then I can't make up my mind in peace."

"But you don't even listen to me. Nobody listens to me."

"I do listen to you. Please, don't let yourself get worked up for no good reason."

She looks at me. I say, "They had said they'd call tomorrow. They should have just called tomorrow."

She suddenly loses it. "What's going to happen between today and tomorrow? The heavens will come down to the earth? Tomorrow is the exact same shit as today. Just say no and let us all off the hook."

She gets up and goes to her medication bag again.

"You know, it's actually none of my business. It's up to you and your father."

I can't control myself anymore.

"That's enough, Mom. Stop shouting. You are terrifying Mahan."

"Mahan, Mahan, he doesn't even know what it means to be terrified."

I swallow the lump in my throat. I mustn't cry. How can I cry when all of this is my fault? I go back to our room. Mahan is still talking on the phone up and laughing. Clearly he hasn't heard Mom's voice. When he notices me walk into the room, he looks up. I say, "Didn't I tell you? She's not mad anymore."

"She's not?"

"No, she's not. Can you please pass me the phone?"

I say hi to Leyla. With laughter in her voice, she asks, "What is it this time?"

"Mom hasn't been feeling well again for some time now. Arsalan's mother called to get an answer on the marriage proposal. I told her we should wait until tomorrow, and she lost it."

"Why do you keep delaying it, Shabaneh? Hurry up, so we can have a wedding before Roja leaves."

"I have cold feet. I'm terrified. I keep thinking about Mahan, about Mom not feeling well, about all the hassle of putting together a wedding. And I don't know whether I love Arsalan enough to actually marry him."

"When you get here, we can talk about it again, for the hundredth time. When are you coming?"

"I came home early to change and head to your place, but this happened the moment I got in. Dad isn't home yet to look after Mahan. I'll wait for him and then I'll come. Is Samira already there?"

"Her flight arrives late tonight. Whenever she visits Iran, she stays in Ahwaz as long as she can. I've done all the grocery shopping, but I feel intimidated by the cooking. I haven't had this many guests in more than a year."

"Don't worry. I'll come over, and we'll do everything together. Good cooking skills are not like the rules of thermodynamics that you can forget over time."

I should leave soon, before Leyla gets more anxious. She's only recently begun to feel better. She is well enough now that she can throw parties like when Misagh was here. We used to get together at their place every weekend and chat all the way into the night. I would put Mahan to bed, and the party would just get rolling. Leyla played the piano, Misagh read stories, and Roja made us all laugh. Misagh and Roja made big plans for getting a PhD and becoming professors and other such things. Leyla's home was the home of my dreams. A home where the man, like Misagh, understands everything, never gets angry, never curses, says stupid things, or bullies, and always looks after his wife. Mahan has withdrawn into himself and is biting his fingernails. I look at my own bitten, uneven fingernails and stop myself from telling him to take his hand out of his mouth. I let him calm himself any way that works for him. I call out to him. He hides his hand behind him and stares at me uneasily. I smile at him to show him I'm not going to scold him for biting his nails. I ask, "Do you know when Dad's going to be home?"

"No. He went out to get Mom's medication and some fruit. He didn't take me along even though I insisted."

I wish Dad were home. If he were, he would say something, and everything would be resolved. He would tell Mom to stop, and then he would turn to me and say, "It's nothing. You don't need to worry. This is what she does every day. She'll recover before you know it. Go take a stroll and refresh your mind." I wish he would come back right away. I don't want to leave Mahan alone with Mom.

Notifications pop up on my phone screen. Arsalan has called twice, but I didn't hear my phone. My bad luck. He might have called while Mahan was on the phone with Leyla. Hopefully he'll believe me when I tell him I wasn't intentionally ignoring his calls and he won't start a fight again. I wish I could just not call him back. I would not call and later I would say, "It is what it is. I didn't want to call. Do you have a problem with that?" Mahan is lying on the bed and browsing through one of his Tintin books. I sit on the chair and dial Arsalan's number. Something keeps pounding left and right on the walls of my heart. I wish he would not pick up. I wish he was not there. I wish I could just hang up. He picks up. Even before I can say hi, he says, "Why didn't you answer your phone, Shabaneh?"

"I'm sorry. Mahan was talking to Leyla on my phone."

"Why didn't you give my mom an answer? Sometimes I feel like you know perfectly well that your behavior humiliates me and you keep doing it on purpose. What are you trying to say that you can't just go ahead and tell me directly? You don't want me? Am I a bad guy? Am I ugly? Am I a dirty bastard? Why don't you just talk to me like a normal human being? What's your problem with me that you keep doing this to me?"

This really is beyond me. I don't have any strength left. I shrink further and further. I become a little, lonely Shabaneh and get lost in a large plain full of wolves where there is no one to rescue me. The wolves attack me. I watch my hand getting ripped apart. I watch a wolf grabbing it with his teeth and running away. My leg is chewed off by another wolf. My waist by another. Then all of them together put their teeth on my throat and squeeze hard until blood splashes all over their eyes. My chin trembles. My tears drop down my cheeks, one by one, and soak my collar. I look at Mahan, who is still busy leafing through his book and does not notice me. I get up and turn toward the wall so that he doesn't see my tears. Arsalan says, "I'm coming over. I'll call you when I get there. Come downstairs so we can talk. Whatever it is needs to come out in the clear today. I'm fed up with all this."

I hold my chin in my hand to stop it from trembling. I gather all my strength and say, "But Arsalan, your mom was supposed to call tomorrow . . ."

"It's not about today or tomorrow or an answer or whatever the hell it is you're saying. My problem is something else. Why are you crying? Wait. I'll be there in half an hour."

"Please, Arsalan. Not today. Just one day . . ."

He shouts, "Fuck this life. This can't be it. You don't even utter a word to let me know what's really wrong with you. Am I just a useless piece of shit in your life?"

He hangs up. I tell myself, Let it go, Shabaneh. Leave it alone for only an hour. Nothing bad is going to happen. I swallow one of Leyla's green pills and wipe my tears off my face. I listen. I can't hear Mom crying in the living room anymore. Mahan has dozed off with his Tintin book over his face. I get up and look at him. His chest moves up and down smoothly. I pick the book up and pull his blanket over him. The weather is getting cooler. I should have asked him if he had lunch. What if he's hungry?

Why does everything go wrong all at the same time? Why can't bad things come my way one by one, so I can have the chance to gather the scattered bits and pieces of myself from around the big plain full of wolves? I sit on the bed. I should find a solution for the mess I've made. I should call Arsalan and make it up to him. We can't stay mad at each other. It's not his fault that I don't love him. He is a good guy. Everyone says so. If he weren't, Roja would know, and she wouldn't let me get together with him. Leyla too would pick up on it. If he were a bad guy, Dad would have noticed it when he came to our house last week with his mother to ask for my hand in marriage. When they left, Dad said, "They seem to be respectable people. But it's your decision, my darling. You know best what to do." But why don't I know best? Why did I pretend I didn't hear what he said the day we went to Jamshidiyeh Park and had ice cream, when he told me he wanted to come to our house with his mother to ask my father for my hand? He said we would set the date soon. And I said, "Okay, I'll tell Dad." But I didn't. I didn't even tell Leyla and Roja. I kept telling myself that nothing had happened that evening, so much so that I began to believe it myself, as if I had dreamed it all. That was not how one asked for someone's hand. So listlessly? So unceremoniously? Arsalan was not wearing a crimson velvet cape that night. I was not wearing a princess dress with a puffy skirt, like what the women wear in Tolstoy's novels. We were sitting in his car, in our work clothes, and as we drove back from the park, instead of holding my hand, smiling, and being gentle, Arsalan kept looking straight at the road, not even looking at me. Leyla had told me how Misagh had invited her to a traditional restaurant and arranged with the server to bring, at the end of their dinner, instead of the check, the bouquet of red roses and the ring he had gotten her. Just like in a novel. But Arsalan didn't read books. He had proposed as if he were asking me what corrections our boss had made to my plans, or as if he were asking if I had taken Mahan to his art class. He proposed the way he liked it, only him. Of course, that's how things are. When I'm so inept, things will always turn out the way he wants. Then I told myself maybe he was just joking, but his frown reminded me that he was not. I wished he would forget all about that night. But he didn't. No matter how much I pretended otherwise and the next day in the office walked the long way to avoid him and hid my face behind my computer screen with the excuse of working on the plans, Arsalan was waiting for an answer from that very day on. That evening, when I left the office, he was waiting for me in the car right outside the door. He said, "So?"

I preferred to play dumb than to give him an answer. I put my head in through the open window of his car and said, "So what?"

"You ask, 'So what?' Are you joking? You're definitely thinking of someone else. Otherwise you wouldn't play me like this."

He pressed his foot on the accelerator and drove away. That evening he didn't give me a ride home. He stopped talking to me and didn't come to work the next day. Roja said, "He's acting up like a spoiled kid. He can't force you to marry him. Don't pay him any attention."

I couldn't do it. When he stopped talking to me, my whole life turned upside down. I couldn't work during the day. I couldn't sleep at night. Wherever I went, I kept hearing my phone buzzing. My stomach churned, and my heart pounded so fast. I felt like when Mahan was a child and he couldn't understand what was going on around him and Mom kept getting upset with us every day; like when I held Mahan tight in my arms and covered his mouth, so no one could hear him crying. I would feed him, and early in the mornings, I would secretly bathe him and wash his pants, so that Mom wouldn't have him admitted at an institution, an institution where the kids weren't washed properly, and the rooms always smelled like pee. Dad smoked and told Mom that he had seen how in the institutions the kids were given pills to sleep all day long, and that at night when they cried, nobody would check on them. He said in the institutions the kids cried themselves to death. He said the kids would call any man who visited Dad, opening their arms to be hugged. He said these things and he broke down crying. He said these things to

Mom in a low voice in their own bedroom, but I could hear him. And I held Mahan tight to my chest in our room and covered his mouth so that nobody would hear him crying and want him to die for us to be relieved of our misery. I was afraid that Mahan would die. My stomach churned, and my heart pounded and felt like boiling up, like the time Arsalan stopped talking to me. I told myself that if he made up with me, just that once, I would listen to and do whatever he said. But he didn't make up with me. He didn't come to work. I was afraid he would resign, and I would feel guilty for the rest of my life over his not having a job.

Leyla said, "Men are proud. How many times do you think he can propose to you? Think this through. Either accept him or be honest with him and tell him that you don't want to marry him."

No matter how hard I tried, I couldn't understand whether she was saying I should accept him or tell him I didn't want him. Roja, too, kept repeating what she always said: "He's not a bad guy, he's just a bit cocky. We need to fix that."

Then she added, "Do you think he'll forget about his job just because of you? You're such a fool. He's having his own fun somewhere else now. All guys are the same. You'll realize later that you're giving yourself a headache for no reason at all."

But I was afraid he would leave his job for me. I was afraid he would leave and not come back. I was afraid that when he left, there would be no one else there to love me. Then I would grow old all by myself and I would be afraid of the dark and cry because of the pain in my legs and there wouldn't be anyone to take me to the doctor. Before he entered my life, I never needed him. I cursed him for appearing out of nowhere and doing something that caused me not to be able to live without him anymore. I cursed him once and I cursed myself a hundred times. Both his presence in my life and his absence were now an issue. I ended up calling his number. I wanted to hang up ten times. But I didn't. While the phone rang, I wanted to throw up all my insides, but when he picked up and gently said hi, everything calmed down inside me all of a sudden. As if all the previous excruciating hours had never been. It was as if I had woken up from the nightmare in which Mahan died. It was as if an earthquake had been trembling my heart, and now it had stopped and no trace of it remained except for a few pieces of plaster dropping from the walls and a photo frame that had fallen on the floor. The half-living, half-dead body of a girl who looked like me pushed the debris aside and pulled herself out. She looked dusty and exhausted, but she was still breathing. She told Arsalan she was going to talk to her father at that very moment, but she was lying. She just wanted Arsalan to make up with her.

I walk out of our room and go check Mom's bedroom. She's wrapped a kerchief around her head and is lying on the bed. The blister packs of her pills are on the bedside table, and I can see she has taken enough that she won't be waking up anytime soon. The apartment gets on my nerves. I need to go to Leyla's. Dad will be back soon. I go back to our room and change quietly so as to not wake up Mahan. I throw my phone in my backpack and close the front door gently and walk downstairs. The cool, cloudy weather outside washes all the bad things from inside our home away. I feel like Edmond Dantès, freed from prison after fourteen years and heading to the island of Monte Cristo with a treasure map in his hand. I like to walk and imagine beautiful stories for myself. I throw the second strap of my backpack onto my shoulder and get going. I become my own little daughter and I am walking back home from school. When I get home, Mom is in a good mood, and like the mothers in kids' cartoons, she smiles at me and embraces me. She then asks me what I would like to eat, and she makes me the very dish I've asked for. We then sit down to chat and play until Dad gets home. I wish I knew what my daughter's father looks like. He is not like the fat man who is opening his front door with a key or like the tall man who's bought some fresh bread and is walking down the alley. No, he's not like any of them. But he's not like Arsalan either. A wind lifts my headscarf and almost blows it away.

Mom had taken me up in her arms and said, "If you don't love your little brother, the wind will blow him away." I felt terrified. I've always been terrified that if I don't love someone enough, the wind will blow them away. As if my love for them would turn into a rock tied to their feet and weigh them down, not letting them budge. Now I'm afraid that if I don't love Arsalan, he'll be blown away by the wind. Then I will be left alone and die of loneliness. Maybe it's been because of this fear of the wind that I've always loved Mahan so much. Even though he never stopped crying, was always in a bad mood, never understood anything, and made Mom upset. Even during those first few days when he was all pinkish and had black hair and cried, I loved him. He had just come home from the hospital with Mom and was always in her arms. He was either having milk or sleeping. I still didn't know what color his eyes were. I told Mom, "Can I hold him for a second?"

"Shh! Your brother has just fallen asleep. Go ahead and hold Suzi instead."

I didn't like Suzi. She was stiff, and one of her arms had broken off and gotten lost. I wanted to hold Mahan, who was soft and pink and moved. I told Dad, "I want to hold him."

Mom said, "Don't pester him, Shabaneh. If you don't love him, the wind will blow him away."

Dad said, "She does love him. Of course she loves him."

Then he told me to sit down. I sat down cross-legged in front of him, the way he was sitting, and bounced my knees up and down out of sheer joy. Dad took Mahan and put him in my lap. He was heavy and soft. My skirt had slipped to the side and his head was on my knee. His hair touched my skin and I felt a shiver. Mahan grumbled and moved his head. His soft, wet black hair rubbed on my skin. I felt a tingle. I pulled my knee back. His head slid down my leg and hit the floor. It made a noise as if it were a ball. Mahan screamed.

A taxi driver honks as he approaches me. I feel disoriented and don't gesture for him to stop. He stops anyway. It's only after I get in that I can bring myself to say, "The square?" A man in the front seat is dozing off. There's no one else in the back seat. I tuck myself all the way behind the driver's seat and hold my backpack in my lap. The driver honks at all the pedestrians waiting at the curb and brakes suddenly, cursing anyone who doesn't get in. He is Arsalan, who has grown old, become a cab driver, and has a fight with everyone in the street, exactly like now. A war has broken out. We've both lost our jobs. I go to Leyla's house in the morning as a maid, because she still has money. Arsalan gets in his dirty green Saipa Pride, which is pretty beaten up, and drives around picking up passengers. I lean against the door even harder and grasp my backpack even tighter. The driver honks again and brakes. The door opens, and a woman pushes a purse and a big bag onto the back seat and gets in. The driver nags under his breath, and before the woman has closed the door all the way, he gets going. I pull the woman's bags toward me so that she has more room to sit. She thanks me. I glance at her. Her face looks weary and sagging, as if she's been crying. She looks like Mom, when, carrying a big bag of Mahan's clothes and diapers, she held on to an envelope including the results of Mahan's CT scans and sat down in Dad's car. I checked the envelope from the back seat and imagined that inside it there was a big piece of paper with a big "Shabaneh" written over it. I still imagine that inside all the big envelopes there is a piece of paper that reads, "All the bad things in the world are Shabaneh's fault." The doctor had asked them, "In the past two years, did he ever fall from a high place? Has there been an incident in which he received a blow to his head?"

Mom picked Mahan up from the examining table and looked at me. I looked down. I was sitting next to Dad. I stopped swinging my pink shoes in the air. I smoothed out the creases in my skirt and wished I could run out of the doctor's office. Mom said, "When he was only three days old . . . his sister's knee."

Dad growled at her, "That wasn't even ten centimeters high. His head slid off his sister's knee, while she was sitting cross-legged on the floor, and gently hit the ground."

The doctor said, "No. I mean hard blows. Like plunging down from some height. Any particular illnesses during your pregnancy?"

"No."

"Did he experience any high fevers when he was a baby? Any convulsions?"

"He did have high fever once. The day the missiles hit the Gisha neighborhood."

"That could be the cause. Do you have a family history of mental disability?"

Mental disability. The words froze in the air and remained suspended there forever. The doctor said we had to do X-rays of Mahan's head. It was wartime, the weather was hot, and no hospital would do X-rays of Mahan's head. Mahan just lay there in Mom's arms in the front seat, with a blank face and lifeless eyes. I would sink in the back seat and look at Mahan, staying quiet the way Mom had told me to. Dad would take a ration coupon from his bag of coupons and fill up the gas, and we would drive from one hospital to another. Dad would run ahead of us and beg the receptionists sitting in their kiosks behind glass windows. Mom would hold Mahan in her arms and walk past people who were screaming in the hospital hallways. Mahan's shoes dirtied Mom's black manteau, and nobody took notice of me holding Suzi tight and running fast after them. Eventually, one day, when the sun went down, we did the X-ray in a gray hospital full of bearded men with a very foul-tempered nurse. That night, lying in my bed, I heard Mom's voice from their bedroom telling Dad, "Would it show in the X-rays if it was Shabaneh's fault?"

I got up and went to the living room and stared at the envelope with the X-ray results until dawn. I thought of taking the envelope and throwing it into the dumpster behind our apartment. I thought and thought and I threw up whatever dinner I'd had and developed a fever. The next morning, when we went to the hospital, Dad held me in his arms and Mom held Mahan.

When I get out of the cab, the fall evening's orange sky, filled with purple clouds spreading out over the end of Leyla's street, makes me feel relieved. Leyla's "Yes?" on the buzzer resonates with such joy that it's as if we are still sophomores and Misagh has called out to her after class by the stairs in front of the campus library. We had just stepped onto the first step when he said, "You play very well."

He had heard her play the piano in the auditorium. The film club was showing *Rashomon*, and Roja had taken Leyla and me along to the screening. We had gone in early so that Roja could check the projector. Leyla noticed the royal piano at the corner of the room and sat down behind it. When Misagh came in to test the audio for the film, he stood in the aisle and wouldn't let anyone test the speakers until Leyla was done playing.

Standing below the steps in front of the library, Misagh had looked up at me and Roja standing like bodyguards by Leyla's side. He had smiled and said, "Roja never said anything about having a musician friend. It's been such a long time since I heard anyone playing Anna Magdalena Bach so well."

I couldn't tell whether Leyla was blushing out of embarrassment or out of joy. Looking at her, only at her, Misagh added, "We have a book club with some of the guys from the student union. Wednesday evenings at the auditorium. It would be our pleasure if you could join us with Roja and your other friend."

When Misagh walked away, we ran after Leyla into the first empty classroom. All the blood in her body had rushed to her face, and like a crazy person, she couldn't stop pacing around the seats. Roja laughed out loud at her. She pointed at her and told me, "She has gone crazy. Look at her. Totally crazy. Here is a lesson for you: never ever do such a thing to yourself!"

Someone laughs out loud in the apartment on the first floor. I walk up the stairs. Many of the leaves of the large rubber fig I had gotten Leyla and placed on the staircase landing have fallen to the floor. She opens the door for me.

"You forgot to water this poor plant again?"

"Oh, I'm sorry. You should remind me, Shabaneh. Come on in. I told you a hundred times that I don't know how to care for plants. You should take it home with you."

"I'll remind you. Let it stay here. It'll cheer you up whenever you get home."

She is in a good mood tonight. I can tell from the red dress she's wearing and the way she has let her light brown hair fall loose on her shoulders. From her house that sparkles. From everything being in its place. From the red rose she's put on the table. From all the windows she has opened, all the lights she has turned on. It's been so long since this many of her light bulbs were actually working. The only mess is in the kitchen, where the table is covered with grocery bags. In her red dress, she keeps moving around the apartment, rushing to put away the things she has bought in the cabinets. She is arranging everything with such order and taste. She looks like her old self. Like when she felt well.

"Did you change the light bulbs yourself? That's a lot of groceries for only a few people!"

She swirls around, and the air dances in her hair and her dress.

"I have guests after such a long time."

Her eyes twinkle. She says, "Aren't you growing tired of this backpack? How many times do I have to tell you it isn't right for your age? You should carry a chic purse like a lady. I made watermelon juice. Do you want some?"

"Let's start cooking. I have to get back home soon. Things are not okay."

Why did I even mention that? What's the use when things are never okay in our home? Leyla puts a glass of watermelon juice on the table and opens one of the grocery bags. I throw my manteau and headscarf over the arm of the red couch. The apartment is so tidy that my manteau on the couch makes it look messy. I notice the corner of the room. The fallboard of the piano is up. I feel breathless out of sheer joy. I haven't heard Leyla play the piano since last winter.

"Have you started playing again?"

Her eyes twinkle again. A flight of tiny birds begins jumping around in them. She says, "It was very hard for me, Shabaneh. But I finally managed to open my piano to see if I can still play. I think it needs to be tuned."

She fills the sink with water and empties the package of mushrooms into it.

"Did you tell Arsalan about tomorrow night?"

I go and stand next to her. She takes the mushrooms out of the water one by one and murmurs a familiar song under her breath as she washes them. I can't remember the song no matter how hard I try. I say, "Let me wash them with a sponge."

"You haven't told Arsalan? No? Why haven't you?"

"I don't know, Leyla. I'm thinking that I might say no."

"Shabaneh, invite him over. Even if you plan on giving him no for an answer, that doesn't mean you can't bring him to the party. At least we can see how he behaves around others. Why don't you ever show him to anyone?"

I run the sponge over the whiteness of the mushrooms, and the coldness of the water on my hand calms me down. She asks, "Should I put the chicken in the freezer?"

"No, come, you wash these mushrooms, I'll cut the chicken. You know I don't like showing Arsalan to anyone. I'm constantly worried that if he does something bad, I'll lose face in front of everyone."

"But he is such a nice person in groups. That night when we went to Farahzad, you could easily tell he was a nice and warm guy you can have lots of fun with. Don't you remember how much we laughed because he kept teasing Roja?"

I give her the sponge and dry my hands. She keeps murmuring the same song. It's not a sad tune, but I don't know why it makes me sad. I say, "I'm so tired, Leyla. I wish he had never come into my life."

My face feels hot. Something boils up in my heart, comes up to my face, and makes my eyes water. I keep talking about sad things and making Leyla feel bad. I can't hold back my tears. I hide them from Leyla. I take an onion from the cabinet under the sink. I skin it and begin chopping; now I can cry without worrying about it. I should make up my mind about everything. I have to settle things today. That's enough. I grab a tissue and say, "I'm not sure about anything. I haven't been from the very beginning. Even last week when he came with his mom to ask for my hand and everyone seemed happy, I had my doubts. Even Mom was happy that day. Can you believe that? Even my Mom. There's something wrong that doesn't let me feel happy. Something bad, something wrong, I don't know. You were always so happy back then. I remember."

"Me? Yes. I was truly happy."

She turns off the water. Fuck it. Why did I remind her of Misagh? She is beginning to forget him. She is beginning to feel well again. She has stopped constantly bringing him up, and his stuff isn't around the apartment anymore. His slippers aren't by the door, and his beret isn't hanging from the coat hanger anymore. She even removed his framed pictures. I press the tissue over my eyes and look up at her. She is wiping her eyes too. She says, "The onion is too strong."

I add the onions to the skillet and put the chicken fillets on the cutting board. Leyla comes and stands in front of me. She is waiting for me to speak. I should talk to her. I say, "This is my last chance. I imagined I would marry with love and excitement, and then all the bad things would come to an end. I imagined everything would be put in place, and my life wouldn't be what it is now anymore. But nothing will get fixed like this. It might even get worse. If I'm separated from Mahan, how is he going to live with Mom?"

"Does Arsalan have a temper? Does he hurt you?"

"No, but he's not nice either. He's very stubborn and too full of himself. He doesn't have big dreams. He's not going to get creative in life; in a hundred years, his life will be exactly the same as it is today. All his days are the same, and he doesn't feel like he needs to change anything. I wish we could sit and read books together and chat about them or watch films together. Or leave for Yush in the middle of the night to go see the poet Nima's house. But Arsalan is not into any of these things. He just likes to joke around and make pointless group plans, go to Farahzad, or go north and smoke hookah all day long and lie around. I don't know what he thinks about. He's just a regular guy. It's bad to just be regular."

She opens the fridge and pours some water for herself. In a low voice, she says, "It's not bad to be a regular person. It's actually good. It's very good that all his days look the same. You can predict where he is going to be tomorrow or the day after or ten years from now. He doesn't read books, but instead he has his feet on the ground. He won't abandon you."

She puts her glass on the counter and sighs. I've made her sad. I should go home. Not like this, though; I need to make Leyla feel better before I go. I say, "Can you chop the mushrooms, please?"

"We've all grown up, Shabaneh. The time for our big dreams and foolish joys is over. What do you think life should be like? It's just a bunch of small, regular things. If we are to be happy, we have to be happy with the small things."

I stir the onions and add the chopped chicken fillets to them.

"How is the newspaper going?"

"The newspaper is going well. It is going very well, actually."

"I can tell. Did you buy just this one package of mushrooms?"

"Do we need more?"

"I'll go get more."

"Roja said she'd come over later tonight. I'll tell her to get another one on her way."

"She said she would come? I hope she does. In the end, I didn't find out what was wrong with her today."

I follow Leyla with my eyes. She is putting the kettle on the stove and turning the burner on. I take the turmeric from the cabinet and sprinkle it over the chicken. I turn the heat lower and put the skillet lid on. Leyla empties a bag of pink gelatin powder into a bowl. She is definitely well if she wants to make Jell-O. She says, "I couldn't figure it out either. This morning, I asked her to come over tonight, but she said she didn't know if she could make it. She seemed in low spirits. I thought it was something at work."

"If it was something at work, she would've told me. She came in today but left early. She said she had a few things she needed to take care of but didn't say what."

I arrange the cold cuts on the chopping board and struggle to unscrew the pickle jar. I can't do it. I hold it out to Leyla, who is pouring the boiling water into the bowl of Jell-O.

"Can you open this?"

She tugs hard, but she can't open it either. She says, "I'll ask Roja to open it when she gets here."

She picks up her phone and dials Roja's number. I add cold water to the Jell-O and put the bowl in the fridge. She says, "Roja isn't picking up. While you're slicing the cold cuts, I'm going to get more mushrooms. Give me the jar too. I'll have Rahman unscrew it. Can I wear your manteau?"

She doesn't wait for my answer and wears it. It's too big for her. When she gets to the door, she turns around and looks at me. Her gaze lasts a thousand years, and then she says, "Just one thing, Shabaneh. Being alone is very hard. It is harder than living with no dreams. You can't live in the clouds forever. Little by little, you come down to earth, and then being alone becomes the hardest thing in the world. Do you understand what I'm saying?"

She closes the door and walks out. I don't understand. Life is hard anyway; every day is harder than the day before. I do live in the clouds. I've become melancholic. These books have made me melancholic. I know. These books full of heroes. Poisonous heroes I kept blending together in my mind, making them bigger or smaller, giving them this quality or that quality, until I ended up creating a hero for myself that can't be found anywhere. Nobody mounts on a horse anymore so that I can stand by a tent and hold on to his horse's reins, pour some hot tea for him, and listen to him talk as he drinks. Nobody comes back beaten and bloody from a fight with the bad guys to be comforted by his wife. Nobody saves his lover from the claws of a dragon in a faraway fort. Nobody is Rostam or Arash or Pouria anymore. Why don't these heroes let me be? Why don't they let me climb down from the clouds and put my feet on the ground in real life? Why do they make me melancholic? Why isn't Arsalan calling? Something pounds itself on the walls of my heart once more. What if he's mad at me again? I should call him myself. Leyla is right. Being alone is hard. It's even hard for Leyla. No matter how good her job is, how good their newsroom is, how good her life is, it's still hard for her to be alone. It's so hard that she has put her mattress on the floor and doesn't sleep in their bed anymore. I can see through her bedroom door.

I had picked up the bedding from the floor and asked her, "Do you have back pain? Is that why you sleep on the floor?"

She sat down on the bed and burst into tears. Roja gave her a tissue and said, "Listen to me. You should throw away this fucking bed."

"I can't."

"Then put it in the storage so that it's not in your face all the time. Are you a masochist?"

The song Leyla was singing keeps playing in my head. I finally remember what it is. It is the piece she practiced for the student union's event. Misagh was the head of the union that year. Leyla's performance was the following morning, and she was nervous. Misagh had asked us to come over and stay with them for the night. Roja hadn't come; she had said Ramin wasn't home, and she had to stay with her mother. I was sitting on the red couch and had the blanket pulled all the way up over me, and no matter how hard I tried, I could not tell which part of the song she was playing well and which part still needed work. But Misagh sat on the floor by the piano all night long and listened carefully a thousand times to what Leyla was playing and praised her playing a thousand times and told her which sections she should play more slowly and which sections more firmly. Until the sun came up. I can hear the key turning. It's Leyla. She bought more mushrooms and mayo. I wash the smell of the cold cuts off my hands and take the jar of pickles from her. She says, "Whether you write a shopping list beforehand and review it a hundred times or not, in the end you always forget something. I had forgotten the mayo. Roja called. She said she's going to come for a bit."

"Arsalan didn't call."

"Call him yourself. And tell him to come tomorrow."

How assured she sounds when she tells me to call and tell him to come. She leaves my manteau on the couch and empties the new package of mushrooms in the sink. I take my phone from my bag and feel nauseated once again. Leyla turns on the water and says, "Call him, Shabaneh."

I sit on the arm of the couch and dial his number. He picks up after the first ring.

"Finally! I've been waiting for hours for your call."

My nausea calms down. I run my hand over the sharpness of the leaf of the fresh red rose on the table.

"You were waiting for me to call?"

"Of course. What's going on? Should I come pick you up?"

"No, I'm at Leyla's."

He gets annoyed. "So that's why you disappeared on me," he says and then goes quiet.

Another Shabaneh, who is not me, hovers over my heart and doesn't let me speak. I get up. Leyla comes and stands in front of me. She mouths silently, "Did you tell him?"

I gesture no with my head. Arsalan says, "Okay, go. You seem busy."

Leyla extends her arm toward me. I can't think straight and hand her my phone.

"Hi, Arsalan. How are you? . . . I wanted to invite you tomorrow night. A few of us are getting together at my place. It would be great if you could join . . . No, don't even mention it. Do you want to talk to Shabaneh? . . . Okay. I'll see you then."

She hangs up and puts my phone on the table. She says, "See? All done."

"Did he say he would come?"

"Yes, why shouldn't he? What kind of food does he like so we can make it for him?"

"Arsalan? I don't know. I was thinking . . . it's true that he doesn't read books, but he never stops me from reading. That is good, right? And who am I? I myself am just a regular, apathetic person too, like many others. Can you tell which one matters more for a couple, that they agree on the big things or the small things? I can't seem to figure it out, no matter how hard I try to think about it."

She looks at me. She gets it. I can tell she gets it. She says, "Don't be so hard on yourself, Shabaneh. No one can force you to do something that you don't want to do. Let him come tomorrow night. Then we can discuss it again after the party. Do you want me to call my therapist and make you an appointment?

The buzzer rings. Leyla gets up.

"That should be Roja."

I don't want to go see Leyla's therapist. I want everything to become clear this very night. I'm tired of being so uncertain. Of being afraid, of being incompetent, of always being at fault for everything. Of not being able to decide for myself like everyone else. I wish I were Comtesse du Barry, and that Louis XV would come and finally marry me. He was the king, so I would have to follow his orders. He was the king, and nobody could talk over what he said, nobody, not even me.

Roja leans on the doorframe to steady herself. I don't recognize her. Her clothes are dusty. There are dark bags under her eyes that never existed there before. She looks pale; she is not wearing lipstick or mascara. She looked better yesterday. I get up. She hands Leyla the bag she has in hand right there at the door.

"Mom made you some grilled eggplants. She said she's already added in the tomatoes and spices. You just have to add four eggs and you'll have your mirza ghasemi ready."

She turns to me.

"You can't even open a pickle jar between the two of you?"

She smiles, but the smile disappears immediately from her face, and a moment later I can't find it there anymore. Leyla says, "Why did you let her cook with her bad back? I'll call and thank her. How are you doing? What's going on?"

"Nothing."

"Then why do you look like this? Come on in."

"No, I have to go. How are you, Shabaneh?"

I'm stunned. I take a step forward and look into her eyes. They are empty. If only she cried, if only she cried a little bit, the skin around her eyes wouldn't get bruised with the weight of her tears. Roja can't feel bad, because she always has to be there for Leyla and me. She asks, "What's new?"

"Nothing. Why do you have to leave so early?"

"I have a few things I need to take care of."

Leyla says, "Come sit for a second. I've been so worried about you."

"Worried? There's nothing wrong with me. I'm just a bit tired. I think I'm getting sick or something. The weather is getting cold. Shabaneh, are you staying the night? It's late. I can give you a lift home if you want."

I have to go home. Mahan is alone. When I'm not home, he gets frightened. I turn to Leyla.

"Is it okay if I go, Leyla? Mom isn't feeling well. I'm afraid if I go back late, she might get grumpy and give me a hard time for tomorrow night."

"Sure, go ahead. Maybe on the way Roja will open up and tell you what's going on with her."

Roja laughs, but the laughter doesn't sit well on her face. "You two are crazy, always worrying!"

I tell Leyla, "Don't touch anything. The chicken fillets will be done in ten minutes. You can just turn it off. I'll add the cream tomorrow so that it's fresh. Just put the mushrooms and everything else I chopped in Tupperware and leave them in the fridge. I'll do everything else tomorrow. I'll arrange the candles as well."

"I have to be at the paper until early evening tomorrow. Samira arrives tonight and is going to visit her friend in the morning. If I give you the key, can the two of you come over a bit earlier?"

I tell her I'll do it. When she hands me the key, she looks into my eyes and says in a low voice that only I can hear, "Don't worry. Everything will resolve itself sooner than you think."

She smiles the most hopeless smile in the world. She too, like me, knows that nothing is ever going to get resolved.

I get in Roja's car and put my backpack on my lap. When she turns the key, her music doesn't fill the car like usual. I am terrified of her mood today and withdraw into myself. The car gets moving, and the cool wind of the beginning of fall blows into the car. Past the traffic light, she asks, "What have you done to Arsalan this time?"

"Nothing. He was the one who got upset. Did Leyla tell you something?"

"No, he called me. He is right, Shabaneh. He is totally right. You can't keep him hanging like this."

Why has he called Roja again? I feel ashamed and keep staring at my dirty shoes, which I forgot to clean again. Arsalan doesn't consider anything. He embarrasses me all the time. I say, "I don't want to keep him hanging, believe me. I'm more tired than anyone else and I know I should settle things sooner rather than later. The problem is the more I think about it, the more certain I am that I don't really love him. Even people who marry when they're in love end up badly. Think of Misagh. He was so good, so kind, he loved Leyla so much, he paid attention to everything. What came of that? In the end, he left Leyla, and look what that did to her. They even knew how to live life. We don't. Arsalan is not like Misagh. He doesn't have half the passion Misagh had. He cannot be gentle. And my situation is not like Leyla's. I have a thousand problems. My mom, Mahan, my own shortcomings. If Leyla's life got ruined like this, of course mine won't turn out well. I'll surely end up worse than Leyla."

"Is that your problem, Shabaneh? Are you afraid that you might end up like Leyla?"

I hold on to my backpack even tighter and look outside my window.

"That's one of my problems."

"Do you want me to tell you why Leyla didn't leave? If I tell you, will you stop this nonsense?"

I turn toward Roja. She signals and makes a turn.

"Our lives are not all in our own hands, Shabaneh. You can only live your own part right. The rest is in other people's hands."

She doesn't look at me. Why didn't Leyla leave? I try to think. All the scenes from Leyla's life bundle together and march in front of my eyes, as if a film on double speed. I do not get it. My mind is not working. I ask Roja, "Is there something I don't know?"

"Leyla did want to go, but she couldn't. When Misagh was all set to leave, and Leyla realized that he really was going, she decided to go with him. But it was too late. She did everything she could, but no school would admit her that late in the year. She didn't tell any of this to anyone, not even to Misagh."

I'm shocked. Roja looks at me. Her eyes are nothing but empty sockets. I murmur, "How do you know?"

"Misagh used to talk to me. One of his last days, he saw all her application papers and the responses on Leyla's computer. None of them spoke about it until the day he left."

Roja stops in front of my building. I ask, "So why didn't he stay?"

"Misagh wasn't the type to stay, Shabaneh. He had big dreams.

And Leyla didn't tell him she wanted to leave with him. She wanted Misagh to stay here for her. Leyla should have made up her mind sooner. She should have asked for his help from the very beginning. Then maybe she could have gone. She kept saying, 'He won't leave without me.' She was being too obstinate for her own good. She kept insisting, 'Because I don't want to leave, he shouldn't leave either.' Don't you remember? She was just trying to prove to herself how much Misagh loved her. She was acting like a masochist. She wanted to make herself suffer and cause everyone else to suffer alongside her. Then she kept saying that Misagh didn't really want her to leave. And when he decided that he was going to leave, she asked for a divorce. You know how much Misagh loved her. You remember that he did everything to take her with him, and no matter how hard he tried, she didn't agree to go with him. Leyla didn't leave him any other choice. She was waiting for the day of his departure, imagining that Misagh would think twice about leaving and come back home to her and tell her, 'I'm not going anywhere without you.' She was crazy. She lived in the clouds. Those last days Misagh didn't have time anymore. He had to pick between his dreams and Leyla. He had gone through a lot to be able to leave. Do you understand? Wouldn't you leave if it were you?"

Instead of looking at me, she just sighs, and this means she isn't expecting me to answer. Leyla's life gets all jumbled up in my mind. It dissolves into pieces, and as if it's an AutoCAD design, each piece explodes on a black screen. I don't know Leyla anymore. Roja turns the engine off and continues, "Arsalan is not a bad guy. He is like everyone else. He has some good qualities and some bad qualities. The only thing that matters is that you love him, so you can live with him. I think you do love him. But sit down and think once and for all and give him an answer. It doesn't matter if you don't want him.

Don't be afraid of anything. Leyla and I will always be there for you. We will all grow old together and not let you be alone."

She looks down. I want to tell her, "But you won't be there. You are leaving, and I'll be left alone." I don't say anything. She adds, "We are grotesque women, Shabaneh. We've walked out of our mothers' lives but have not yet walked into our daughters' lives. Our hearts belong to the past, but our minds to the future. Each life pulls us toward itself and tears us into pieces. If we weren't so misshapen, all three of us would be peacefully sitting in our homes right now, raising our kids. We would dedicate all our love and goals and futures to our children, like all women throughout history, and we wouldn't be running after so much nonsense all the time. Leyla would have submitted like a good woman and followed her husband. I wouldn't bring myself so much suffering with all the debt and moneymaking and work and different hardships. I would stay here and just live my life with peace of mind. And you would have your husband and children and be happy. Instead of being Mahan's mom, you would be a mother to your own kids. And on weekends, we would all go get our nails done, and instead of faraway unreachable joys, we would just have fun at our nightly parties and enjoy buying silk dresses during sales. Look at Parastoo. Do you think her life is bad? Do you think she has a hard time with that businessman husband of hers? No, Shabaneh, she doesn't have a hard life. She can stop coming to work whenever she wants to. Without ever worrying about anything, she always has new clothes to wear and goes on a trip for every vacation. Look at us. Look at yourself. Are you really twenty-eight? Do you look as attractive as a twenty-eight-year-old? Your hair, your face, the way you look. Instead of thinking about your own life, you keep thinking about Mahan and your mom and Leyla's life and your senseless dreams."

A sound from a distance calls me, "Shaba, come."

I look up. Mahan is sticking his head out of the window and is calling out to me. Roja gets out of the car and waves at Mahan. Mahan blows her a kiss. Mahan seems so upbeat; Mom has probably calmed down. Roja says, "Go on up, Shabaneh. Maybe tomorrow will be a better day."

I barely regain my voice to say goodbye to her. She pushes her foot on the accelerator and speeds away. I feel heavy. It's as if the whole world has fallen on my chest with all its weight. I drag my heavy self, my incapable self, my forever-defeated self up the stairs. I should settle things. I should settle things tonight. Mahan meets me at the door. He grabs my backpack and makes me disappear in his big hug. I wish Arsalan had arms as large as Mahan's to make me disappear in his hug. We walk in. I say hi. Dad responds without looking up from the book of poems he is reading. Mom is sitting on the couch, pressing her palm on her forehead. I feel like I'm suffocating. I swallow the lump in my throat with a lot of effort and say, "Mom, can you call Arsalan's mother to set things up? Tell her I said yes."

Dad closes his book and puts his glasses on top. Mom takes her hand off her forehead and says, "What am I going to do with this sick child when you are gone?"

THREE

A l'attention de: Autorités consulaires françaises à Téhéran
Objet: Demande de recours d'un visa d'études rejeté

THEY DON'T HAVE ANY INTEGRITY. No integrity whatsoever. I hate this word: *rejeté*. Why me? Why directed at me? I called a hundred times to find out when I would hear back about the visa. I told them to tell me as soon as possible. They said, "There's no time line. You have to wait." I said, "Your 'There's no time line' will ruin my future. What do you mean there's no time line? Classes have already begun." They said I had to wait. They hung up on me. They don't have any integrity.

I can't just give up. I need to sit and think properly. There has to be a way. I have to find a way. It's been two months since classes began. I need to finish this letter of appeal today. It's already late. In two hours, I have to head out to another stupid kid's place to teach him about the greatest common denominator. Then I need to come back home and get ready for Leyla's party. Why hasn't anyone told her this is not the time to throw a party—in the middle of all this. Do you think everything will go back to how it used to be if you just throw a party? She's so naive and stupid. This fucking pen is not working. Where am I going to find a pen on this messy desk? I push the papers aside. There's no pen. I empty the penholder. There's no pen. There is none in any of the drawers either. There's no pen anywhere in this damned desk. I grab the papers from the desk and throw them at the wall. But they don't really hit the wall. They float like the autumn leaves drifting in the street yesterday, swirling around and falling down onto the ground. I stepped on them, crushing them under my feet. My pen is right here, under my fucking work certificate. That's enough. It's already noon. I need to keep calm. I need to sit and think calmly. I have to write a solid letter.

Madame, Monsieur,
J'ai l'honneur de vous écrire pour solliciter votre bienveillance, et le bénéfice d'un deuxième examen de ma demande de visa d'études rejetée.

This doesn't sound right. Such soft language. I wish they could just understand straightforward language. Then I would say, "Madame, Monsieur, I beg of you in the name of whomever you love. Please reconsider my visa. I'm not one to endure such jokes. Since yesterday my heart has been pounding a thousand beats per second. I might have a heart attack. I might die of sorrow." I would ask them, "If you haven't approved my visa, then whose visa have you approved? Who has killed herself for a fucking PhD like I did? Who has devoted their whole life to this goal?" I would even lose my temper. I would say, "You're just a piece of shit to not have approved my visa. You shameless people." My future is turning into ash and smoke in front of my eyes.

I can't write anything like that. My tea has gone cold. I can't drink it anymore. Mom came and left it on my desk. It was early morning. I haven't left my room since I woke up. I knew it was Friday and I didn't have to go to work, but I didn't remember what had happened yesterday. I kept staring at the ceiling, wondering why my head and my entire body ached so badly. I couldn't tell. The song from *Arizona Dream* kept repeating in my head. I realized what had happened, and suddenly, as if there was an earthquake, the room's ceiling collapsed on my body. Then I remembered that I had stayed awake for hours during the night, staring at the wall and the ceiling and the Amélie Poulain poster on my closet door. My legs and teeth ached. Even my hair. Last night I hadn't been sad. I hadn't felt anything at all. I had just been confused. It was as if I wasn't myself. It was as if I had heard that Sayeh's visa had been rejected and had commented, "Oh, poor girl," and then completely forgotten about it. But when I woke up this morning, my heart was pounding so hard. I got up but didn't leave my room. I didn't even wash my face. I didn't even have breakfast. Mom opened the door to my room. She saw that I was awake, sitting at the desk, tugging at my hair with my fist. I had drawn a hundred lines with the blue pen on the papers on my desk. Mom realized that something was wrong, but she didn't ask anything. She knows better. Whenever I'm mad as hell, she doesn't ask anything. She left the tea on my desk and asked, "Do you want breakfast?" I said no. I drew another line. The paper ripped apart. She stood there. I didn't look up. She straightened the carpet's fringes with the tip of her slippers. She was waiting for me to say something. I didn't. She said, "Ramin said he called your cell phone, but it was off. He asked me to tell you that if the roads aren't busy he'll get here by early evening and join you for Leyla's party tonight. Apparently, he didn't find anyone to cover his shift yesterday, so he couldn't leave sooner. The roads aren't that busy Friday mornings, are they?"

"No, I don't think so."

She bent down and picked up the two pieces of paper I had torn up earlier. It didn't matter. She wouldn't know what I had written in French. I heard her crumpling them up in her hand. She kept waiting; I remained silent. Finally, she said, "Did Leyla add eggs to the mirza ghasemi? I should call her and see if she needs anything else I can cook for her, and you can just take it when you go to her place. Poor girl, she has gone to work with all these guests she has. When will you go?"

"I don't know yet."

She closed the door gently and walked away. Why am I taking it all out on her? It's not her fault. Even if her heart was not into me leaving, and no one is going to be as happy as she is that I'm not leaving, she wasn't the one calling them to say they should reject me. I should leave my room and ask her to make me some borage tea. I should calm myself down. I should sit and think properly to understand what has befallen me. I can't stand myself. I told Shabaneh I had a few things I needed to take care of. I lied. I couldn't stand myself. I felt as if my head had been chopped off. Like Hana, grandma's chicken. Grandma had her veil wrapped around her waist. She held Hana's neck and brought its beak under the pool faucet to drink water. Then she put the bird in the waterways around the pool. She put its legs on top of its wings, pulled a knife from under her veil, and cut its neck. Hana flapped its wings and jumped. Its blood splashed on grandma's clothes. She took a step back.

"Damn! Making me impure with your dirty blood."

Yesterday I felt like Hana. I wanted to throw myself to the ground and against the walls and the faucet of the pool until all my feathers were gone. Its blood had splashed all around the courtyard. Mom had run onto the balcony and covered my eyes. She said, "Grandma dear, you cut off the chicken's head in front of a child?!" I got up. Shabaneh said, "Where are you going all of a sudden?" I said I had a few things to take care of. She followed me to the stairs. She asked, "Where are you going? Are you okay?" I said yes, but I was lying. I wasn't okay.

I walked out. I walked around in the streets until evening. I kicked my feet on the ground. I crushed the poor yellow leaves on the ground. I threw them up into the air. Then I sat down on the curb. I tugged at my hair. My short hair kept escaping. I felt like someone had slapped me in the face. I had said, "Madame, it wasn't me." She had said, "Who else can climb up the drainpipe all the way to the roof?" I had said, "I didn't climb it." She had said, "Aren't you ashamed? Can't you see what a mess the ceiling is? It's dripping. The classroom is full of water." She had held my chin in her hand and said, "Why did you put the pigeon's nest in the gutter? Huh?" I had taken a step back and said, "I'm telling you, it wasn't me." And then a loud sound swirled through my ear. Everything became dark in front of my eyes. Mom said, "May her hand be broken." I didn't go to school the next day. No matter how much Mom cried and got mad at me, I didn't budge. She said, "You will end up like Auntie, shut up in the house." I said, "I won't go back to her class." Every day, Mom would pull my arm and take me to school by force. Every day I would run away. I would jump over the school wall and come back home. I couldn't forget the sound of that slap. I stood by the schoolyard wall and clutched my hair in my fist and kept pulling at it. A week later, Mom came to school and changed my class. It was the sound of that very slap that I heard through the phone yesterday. I was sitting at my desk at work. I jumped out of my seat when I saw the embassy's number. I stood facing the window. My heart beat like the heart of Ramin's lovebird when I held it in my hand. It was the same woman I had met with, Shabestari, with the same cold, disgusting voice. The few seconds when she asked for my name and realized it was me she was looking for, time froze and stretched out, the seconds turning into a thousand hours. A thousand hours during which I could count all the persimmons on the trees in front of me or fill out the data for ten tables for Mr. Moghadam. I kept repeating to myself, "Come on, go ahead, tell me. Tell me when I need to come and get my visa. My classes have already started." I wanted to ask her how late the embassy was open. I thought I would just go get it right then. Why leave it till Saturday? I would go get it and then go to a travel agency before they closed at noon on a Thursday and purchase my ticket. I was already far behind the rest of my schoolmates. I should call Ramin and ask him to come stay with Mom, so she doesn't get too restless. Leyla and Shabaneh would come to say their goodbyes too. My suitcase has already been packed for the past two months. She said, "Unfortunately the French government has not approved your student visa."

I was slapped in the face. I froze. I sat down. I felt someone sitting me down. I couldn't say anything. I had to say something. I should have said, "Why are you lying? Why are you playing with me?" I should have said, "What should I do now, with all the days of my life that are going to burn up in front of my eyes and turn into smoke and go to hell?" I should have said, "I don't have anything left to stay here for." I didn't. I couldn't. She said, "If you want, you can write a letter of appeal and fax it to the embassy."

I said okay. That was the only thing I said. The only thing I could say. I need to sit down and finish writing this fucking letter. I should fax it off early tomorrow morning.

Je vous informe que mon dossier de visa était complet accompagné de toutes les pièces nécessaires, mais malheureusement ma demande a été rejetée, et je ne sais pas pourquoi.

I cross it out. That's not good enough. What should I write instead? How should I say this? How can I explain to them what misery has befallen me? I can't think. This is the final step. I should do it well. I pull sample letters out of my bag and line them up in front of me. I printed a dozen of them last night. I didn't know what to write. I hadn't asked Shabestari. When evening came, and my legs felt numb from walking around and I felt like myself again, I called Misagh. To hell with the insane phone bill, even if I don't have any money and am in debt. To hell with not knowing what time it is on the other side of the world and whether Misagh is asleep or awake. I called. He picked up immediately. I said, "Hi, Misagh. What does one write in a letter of appeal?" He was silent. I listened to his breathing. Then he said, "Don't tell me you got rejected!" I tugged at my hair. I said, "Don't ask me anything. Just tell me what I should write." He exhaled and said, "I'm not sure how things work with the French embassy." Then he listened to me and said, "Call Samira." I said, "I can't tell Samira. I don't want to tell anyone." He said, "Tell her." He said, "Talk to someone. Cry. It's okay to cry. Otherwise, you'll go mad." I wish he were here. I wish he would put his hand on my shoulder and tell me, "Don't worry. It's not a big deal. We'll figure a way out." He would say, "Now try this or that." I wish we could sit at their place and talk, talk until we could find a different solution for my life. I'll lose my mind like this.

Then I went to an internet café. There's still one on our street. I sat at the computer. Not that I didn't know where to search, no, but I just kept opening page after page while I thought. Finally, I found samples of letters of appeal. I read a few of them and got a sense of what to write. I should rewrite my statement of purpose. I should write all the steps I've taken so far to prepare to leave. Which ones should I pick?

"Roja . . ."

It's Mom. She stands behind the closed door. She can tell that I'm mad as hell today.

"Come on in, Mom."

She opens the door.

"Here you go. Put these in your suitcase."

She is holding a small box. She puts it on my desk. When she opens the lid, a familiar scent fills the room.

"I've put them in the box so they don't scatter in your suitcase and mess up your clothes. Why is it so dark in here?"

She leaves the box on my desk and draws back the dark blue curtains. The light pours in. I'm in no mood for the light. I was hiding in the dark. I look down. She must not see my eyes. If she sees them, she'll know what's going on. She must not know. The light brightens up the box. It contains six little glass jars full of spices. She says, "I bought the jars yesterday. Aren't they pretty?"

They are pretty, even if my mouth doesn't open to say so.

"Put it in your suitcase now so that you don't forget it. And get up and let me size up your sweater against you. If it fits, I can finish it today, so you can just take it with you. I wanted to give it to Leyla to mail it to you later, but it's better this way."

I get up. She puts the pieces of the sweater over my torso. She takes two steps back and looks at me. Her eyes sparkle.

"Purple looks so good on you."

She grabs the sweater pieces, and as she's closing the door behind her, she says, "Will you have time to go get some fish so that I can cook it for Ramin tomorrow?"

"Sure."

"And lunch is ready. Whenever you want to eat, just let me know."

I pick up the box. It smells of a thousand good old scents blending together. The scent of the upper cabinet in our home in Rasht, the scent of Grandpa's store, the scent of Dad's hands, the scent of Dad's clothes. The box pulls me back into Dad's arms. He would deepen his voice and sing, "Who's eating?"

"The king, the king!"

He sat me on his lap.

"Is it fair for the king to eat everything all by himself?"

I jumped off his lap and stomped on the floor four times. Ramin followed along with me. "No, no, no, no."

"Shh!"

Mom brought out Dad's books from under her veil and gave them to him.

"Don't teach such things to the kids, Mohsen. That's dangerous. They might repeat them in front of others."

She folded her veil and added in a low voice, "And don't say them yourself either. We need you alive."

I pull my suitcase out from under my bed. Leyla got it for me as a going-away gift. I asked her, "Isn't this too big?" She said, "No. I've already packed a suitcase for someone leaving. I know how large it needs to be. There are a lot of things you need to take with you." She sighed. I open the lid. My visa will be issued. Of course it will be issued. Everything is ready here. My coats, my scarves, my tights. I push all of them to the side and place the box of spices in a corner of the suitcase. I hide its scent among my clothes. I sit on the floor. How can I tell Mom that I've been rejected? What should I do with all these skirts and hats that are of no use to me here whatsoever?

I had held Leyla's shoulders and pushed her to stand by the wall. "You are not going to move from here. Understood?"

She couldn't stop sobbing. I pulled the sheets off the bed, crumpled them up, and threw them in the trash bag. A corner was left out. I took the picture frames on their bedside tables, along with Misagh's pajamas, which Leyla had still not taken off the bed, and threw them all in the bag as well. I gave it a hard kick.

"You either tell Rahman to come and take away this trash or I'll set fire to it right here. After two weeks, there is no scent left in the fucking sheets. And stop looking at these pictures. You'll go mad."

She slid down the wall and sat right there on the floor. She could not stop sobbing.

"Look, Leyla. Misagh started his classes yesterday. Even if you keep staring at all of this stuff until eternity, he is not going to come back. Get up and pull yourself together."

I should get up and pull myself together. I should throw these clothes out. I should set them on fire. This suitcase under my bed is definitely going to drive me crazy. Why didn't I finish the fucking letter? How is it already two thirty? It was just ten a moment ago. Who was the idiot who said time is linear? He was wrong. Time is a polynomial equation. If you have a letter you need to write or something you need to do, two hours turn into two minutes, or even two seconds. You bat an eye, and they are gone. But if you are waiting, waiting, for example, for the response from a stupid embassy employee, two months turn into two hundred years. Your image in the mirror grows older and older. Days snap your life out of your hand without even turning into nights. In half an hour I have to be at

Amir Ali's all the way on the other side of the city for his tutoring session.

I get ready. I don't look in the mirror. What's there to see in such a malevolent face? I pick up my purse. I keep my head down as I walk out. Mom must not see my face. I shout out a goodbye and don't wait for her response. I rush out so that she cannot ask, "Did you have lunch?" or "Why don't you have lunch?" or "When will you have lunch?" She must not find out. No one can find anything out. My visa will definitely be issued. Before anyone can begin talking about it, grilling me, or saying among themselves, "Oh, poor girl, she tried so hard." My visa will be issued.

I turn the car key and shut off the loud, awful voice of Elvis Costello. In this misery, why is it so overcast today? I don't know why everyone kills for the fall weather; it doesn't offer anything other than sludge and overcast skies. All these fake intellectuals with their obnoxious gestures. Leyla kills herself to imitate them too. Why do I feel nauseous? I'm going to kill Amir Ali if he plays dumb in class again today. His IQ has not improved for sure since three days ago. So I definitely am going to kill him. I should have canceled his class. I really don't want to write this bullshit letter today. Already two months have passed since the beginning of the school year; what difference does one more day make? Fuck this. My mind keeps jumping around, from here to there, from our home to the class, from Tehran to Toulouse. These fuckers sat me down on a large swing and every day they push me from one side of the world to the other. I'm neither here nor there. I'm left suspended in the middle of the air. In the past two months, I've been hanging in the air. The day I handed in my documents, it felt like I left along with them. I left here but didn't arrive anywhere. I've been hanging in the air. In the sky. It's hard to be up in the sky. These bastards don't get it.

I turn the engine off. There's no way I'm going to tutor today. If I'm not going to leave for France, why should I go and get annoyed by the ignorance of a stupid kid for two straight hours? Fuck money. How much more am I going to make in these few days of tutoring?

I told Shabaneh, "Didn't he propose? If you're going to get married, he'll probably need his money."

"Are you crazy? Arsalan will never mention it. You shouldn't worry about that money for a long time."

But I'm worried. How can I not be? I haven't yet paid back his five million tomans. The moment I leave Iran, I won't have any money to pay him back. Tomorrow morning I'm going to get my euros from the bank and pay my debt to Arsalan. The rest I'll spend on traveling and shopping and having fun. If my visa is not issued, I'm going to spend the rest of my life living like everyone else. Like my own self in ten years, after I've finished doing whatever I wanted to do in life. And I'm going to stop having big dreams. What is the use of causing myself so much suffering in the end? Just to postpone realizing that I haven't become anyone in life and won't ever? I wish they would just give me an electric shock and I would forget everything. I wish I had no memory at all. I wish I were a fish, the way Dad wanted, and my memory would get reset every day. Then, every morning when I wake up, I will forget that I was supposed to go to France or some other fucking country the day before. I would forget how I took part in the national university entrance exam, how I studied, made money, finished an MS, then got admitted to a school in France. Then, like the character in *Memento,* I would write everything I need on the wall, but I would just write, "Nothing." Every day I would write only that. I would write that I never wanted to gain anything important in my life.

Twenty-four hours later I turn my cell phone on. Ten text

messages come in, one after another. I don't read them. A weak, hesitant rain begins to fall over the windshield. I turn the wipers on, and the windshield gets all muddy and dirty. I call Amir Ali's mother. She is upbeat like usual.

"I sent you the fee for the next four sessions yesterday. Did you get it?"

"Yes, thank you."

"Amir Ali has been driving me nuts all day. He just finished his exercises."

"I'm so sorry, but I can't make it today."

"Oh no, dear Roja, that can't be. Amir Ali has an exam tomorrow."

To hell with his exam. Fuck him and his exam. What does his exam have to do with me? How did we take exams without a father, without money, without anything? I pretend to blow my nose loudly. I say, "I have a cold. If I come, Amir Ali will get sick too. Tell him to do the exercises I already gave him and if he has any questions, he can call me. I have my cell phone on."

Before she can say anything, I hang up. I turn my cell phone off and start to drive. Only a few drops of rain, and once again these streets are all tangled up. The intersection is locked. I speed down onto a side street. At least Ramin didn't sell this beat-up car, and I don't have to stand at the curb waiting for the disgusting cabs that just speed by and splash the shit in the streets all over me. After two years, this is the first time I've canceled Amir Ali's session, and his mother is sure to complain. Stupid woman! The biggest concern of her life is for her lazy son to barely pass his midterm math exam. She doesn't think about the fact that the best her son can do is to just show up at her father's construction sites in ten years, build some thin walls, and rip people off. Why does he need a better grade in math? It would be so nice not to be in need of money. I could just spit in their faces, not go tutor on a Friday afternoon, and sleep in. I would not need to go anywhere, neither to classes, nor to France, nor around the corner, nor any other place. I could just sit by my mom until I grow old. I don't understand where we got this idea of having to become someone. Since when did we begin to think we should become someone or do something? So many people all around the world are living like plants. They get up, they eat, they run around, and they sleep. So what? Dad used to say, "Live in a way that people will remember you after you are gone." I had won the first prize in Gilan's theater competition for young kids. Dad had borrowed Grandpa's car and picked me up. I still hadn't taken off my devil costume. The cape and horns and tail that Mom had made for me tripped me up. Dad had bought me a doll as a present. I had decapitated the doll. I was trying to pull out its eyes through its neck to see why its eyes closed when I laid the doll down. Dad took the doll from me and set it aside. He sat me in front of him and said, "I didn't become anyone in my life, but you and Ramin should. Will you remember that?" I said, "Yes, I'll remember." The following day, he left and never came back. What do I have left of Dad other than these words and his green eyes? He never came back to see that these words of his have ruined my life. He didn't become anyone in life, so why should I?

I honk the horn. Why doesn't this traffic light turn green? What useless, heavy traffic this is on a Friday afternoon. Why can't these people stay home even on a weekend? The car ahead of me also honks at the car ahead of it, and that one at the one ahead. Why do they have to sit at the wheel when they're in such a shitty mood? Two kids suddenly appear out of nowhere and run around among the cars. Smoke rises from the *esfand* they're burning in rusty metal cans. A Kurdish peddler stands at the corner of the intersection, his arms covered in golden and silver watches all the way from his wrist to his upper arm. Everything about him is weirdly terrifying. His turban, his pants, the shawl around his waist, and his eyes. His eyes are the strangest. If he were to speak, his accent too would be strange. If I were to get my visa, I would become just as much of a stranger in France. No matter how I would wear chic clothes, cut my hair like Audrey Tautou, and speak with no accent, I would still remain a stranger. The man at the corner of the intersection keeps standing there and doesn't walk forward. I drive past him. He doesn't fit in these streets. Like a purple button over a brown coat, he is completely out of place here. I'll become out of place in the streets of Toulouse as well. I will not fit in. I will not find a corner that will remind me of something and make my lips curve upward in a smile. I will have to build everything from nothing, from the day I was born. My life's counter will restart from zero there. With no memories whatsoever.

I park in front of Leyla's building. Where else can I go? Because of this fucking France thing I am left with no other friends. I had a thousand friends before. My friends from go-karting, from the film club, from the Iran tourism club. Now it feels like I've turned into an old man, and my ten kids have all left home, leaving behind just me and my wife. I only have Leyla and Shabaneh left. Exactly like when I first arrived from Rasht and I still hadn't gotten attached to anyone in this misshapen gray city other than these two. I buzz a few times. Shabaneh should already be here. She was supposed to come early. Lucky her. Lucky all of them who don't give leaving one fucking thought. When Shabaneh begins chatting, even if she says nonsense, it will help pass this hard day. Mahan's voice says at the buzzer, "Roja, look at my clothes."

I go up. I hope tonight doesn't get too crowded. I wish I held the remote control to everyone in my hand and could not let them ask me anything. Whenever they began to utter a question, I could turn them off, or fast-forward them, or have them explode into pieces. I'm ready to crush the head of the first person who asks anything about my visa or makes a comment about it or tries to sympathize with me or whatever fucking else with a twenty-kilo rock, like the character in *11:14*. Mahan has opened the door and stands there with a wide smile. He looks closely at my face. His smile begins to fade, and he takes a step back. I take his arms in my hands and shake him.

"Wow, you look very handsome tonight!"

He is wearing a blue checkered shirt with khaki pants. He murmurs, "Arsalan got them for me."

Shabaneh walks out of the kitchen. Her hands are wet.

"He picked us up this morning. We went shopping, had lunch, and he dropped us off here. He said he would come join us in two or three hours."

I close the door. Shabaneh looks like she is hiding something.

"He got Mahan these clothes and he got me this."

She opens her wet fist to show me. A fine white gold necklace shines in her palm. What has she done now? I don't know how I look at her that makes her quickly hide the necklace in her fist and go back to the kitchen. There is a bag of cold cuts on the counter, along with a handful of toothpicks and some olives and tomatoes. She says, "Last night I told Mom to call them and get the ball rolling for the engagement. To tell you the truth, I'm tired of this constant uncertainty. Leyla says, 'One learns a lot of things during an engagement. Then you can break it off if you don't want to marry him.'"

"For the past year, you said you would break it off if you decided you didn't want him. Were you able to?"

Mahan bristles at me and stands, like a high wall, between Shabaneh and me.

"Shaba said she didn't want it, but he bought it for her anyway."

"I didn't say anything bad to your sister. Why do you get upset, my love?"

Shabaneh keeps rolling the cold cuts, adding this and that to them on the toothpicks and arranging them on the tray.

"What are you doing, you crazy girl? Don't you have anything better to do? Just place them all next to one another in the tray, and we'll just eat them like that."

"Do you think I made a mistake letting him buy me the necklace, Roja? I didn't know what to do. He would get offended if I didn't accept. I'm worried Mom might get mad at me. I called you a few times to tell you. Why is your phone off?"

I take off my manteau and hang it.

"No particular reason."

"Why do you look so sloppy? Where are your clothes for tonight?"

I look at what I'm wearing. I forgot to change out of my pajama shirt.

"I'll borrow something from Leyla."

Mahan asks me, "Are you sick?"

From the moment I got here, he's been staring at my face. I run my fingers through his straight hair.

"No, sir. I'm just not wearing makeup. That's very nice of you to pay such attention to me."

Shabaneh says, "Pay attention? Poor boy, he has never seen you like this. He's not used to it."

"He'll get used to it."

I get up and punch him playfully in the stomach.

"Come on, get up, let's style your hair in the latest fashion, my love!"

"Can I go, Shaba?"

"We should style your sister's hair, too, when she's done styling the meat. Come on, Mahan."

We go to Leyla's room. I hate Shabaneh's kind, concerned, and searching eyes. I don't want her to look at me like that. Nobody should pity me. I can take care of my own life. Haven't I done so before? Didn't I get everything done that they told me I couldn't do to get my admission? Didn't I sleep only four hours a night for two months to pass that fucking exam that everyone kept telling me I would fail? I went to work every morning at seven, went to teach after work at five in the afternoon, and got home at nine only to start studying French until three in the morning. Leyla said, "You've aged. You are insane. Have you seen the lines around your eyes? You could've gotten time off work at least for the past two months."

"I need the money."

"Then cancel some of your tutoring sessions."

Mom brought us some tea. She thought I didn't know it was she who called Leyla and Misagh to come over and save me. Misagh sighed.

"I wish Leyla had some of your motivation."

I still hadn't taken my exam when Misagh left without Leyla. I sit Mahan at her vanity. I tell him not to move. In a low voice, I ask him, "Do you think I'm going to leave eventually?"

"Where?"

"France, of course."

"To be with Misagh?"

"No, you silly goose. Misagh lives in Canada now."

"Don't go, Roja. It's too far away. You'll get lost. Didn't you see how Misagh got lost?"

A chill whirls around in my body. I get up. The black irises of Mahan's eyes follow me around the room. I look through all of Leyla's drawers. There's no sign of hairspray. What the hell. There are no signs of a woman living here. I find an old jar of gel in the last drawer. Only a bit remains at the bottom. I beat the bottle over my palm. Mahan gets scared and closes his eyes.

Misagh had said, "Open your eyes now."

Leyla had removed her hands from over my eyes. Somebody switched on the lights. Misagh jumped in front of me as if he were a magician. When he opened his fists, confetti filled the air in their apartment. Leyla sat down at the piano. Ramin walked out of the room and stood by the door. Misagh kept laughing loudly. He was wearing a high fedora. He was a magician that night. He stood over Leyla and tapped on the piano top to the tune of "Happy Birthday" as Leyla played the song. Shabaneh came out of the kitchen, carrying a cake full of lit candles. Misagh was behind her, dancing around her, blowing the candles in my place. Shabaneh laughed and said, "Stop doing that, Misagh." He didn't listen. I was still standing at the entrance. Misagh put a birthday hat on my head. Leyla played the song "Why Don't You Dance?" Misagh said, "I wish these nights never came to an end."

I run my fingers through Mahan's soft black hair and push all of it back from his forehead. I empty the last drop of hair gel on my finger and lather it on the hair on top of his head, which already looks like a hedgehog. I pull back a bit and look at him at a distance.

"You look gorgeous. Hurry up, go show it to Shabaneh."

He checks himself out in the mirror. His face brightens up.

"Yes, I do look gorgeous."

He gets up and runs out of the room calling for Shabaneh.

I look at Leyla's bookcase and at the empty space left from Misagh's DVD collection. This is now the only empty space he left behind in the apartment. He only took the movies with him. When he was still here, the room felt brighter. Misagh would sit here, right on this bed. He was wearing the steel-framed glasses Leyla and I had bought for him one day from a peddler at the Friday market and read us stories: "That night there was me, Qasem, the son of Zivar who sold tickets, Ahmad Hussein, and two others who had just befriended us on the platform in front of the bank . . ." Leyla had said the frames would suit him. The peddler was packing up his glasses, watches, compasses, and other paraphernalia to go home. Leyla asked him, "Sir, would it be possible to change the lenses of these frames?" I said, "You don't wear glasses yourself. These frames are not comfortable. They are hard on the ears and the nose." The peddler said, "Yes, they can be changed." Leyla bought the frames and had the lenses changed for Misagh. He wore the glasses and read Gogol and laughed out loud. He would read parts of it for us too. If we didn't burst out laughing, he would get annoyed and make fun of us.

"You should all just go ahead and laugh with that stupid show of yours, *Happy Hour*."

And he would imitate the show's characters being clowns, and we would all burst out laughing. Then we would go to the little balcony of their bedroom to smoke cigarettes, and Misagh, with his arms around Leyla's shoulders, would keep telling me about Chaplin. Their apartment seemed much brighter when Misagh talked.

"Why are you sitting here?"

Shabaneh sits down next to me on the bed.

"I'm wondering what I should wear."

She is restless. She keeps her head down and keeps fumbling with her fingers. She finally says, "You know, Roja, you've always helped me out. But now that you're not feeling well, I don't even know what's going on with you or what I can do to help you. Why don't you ever reach out to me? I know that I'm hopeless, but maybe I could do something for you."

I get up without glancing at her.

"Come on, don't be so sentimental. Is there anything left to do for dinner tonight?"

"Are you mad at me? Is it because of Arsalan? But you never told me what to do about him."

"Have you lost your mind? Why should I be mad at you? Come on. The guests will be here soon. And go ahead and wear some mascara to liven your eyes up a bit."

She gets up. She's on edge. I look at her expectantly. She looks down. In a voice lower than before, she adds, "Just one other thing. I want to ask Arsalan if we can take Mahan to come live with us. The more I think about it, the more I realize that I can't leave him with Mom."

I sit back on the bed. How can anyone be so stupid?

"You know, Roja, Arsalan loves Mahan. I mean he has loved him since the day all of us went to Farahzad together. Do you remember? And today he got him those clothes. Mahan wouldn't be any trouble for us, how could he? He'll just live his own life. Do you think I could ask Arsalan?"

"No, Shabaneh. That's just too much to ask. And it's not logical. And it's not going to be good for your life. There's nothing good about this stupid decision. I don't understand how you come up with such ideas."

Why is my voice so high? I tug at my hair. I'm not feeling well, and Shabaneh keeps talking nonsense and pestering me. A key turns in the front door. Then comes Leyla's low voice praising Mahan's hair and clothes and kissing him. Shabaneh looks at me. Her eyes are sparkling with tears. She says, "You're right. I can never think straight."

"You're mad and keep hallucinating. Tomorrow, you'll laugh at your own words. Leyla is here. Shall we go?"

She stares at the ceiling with her eyes full of tears and keeps batting her eyelashes. She inhales deeply. Only Shabaneh knows how to return her tears back into her eyes.

Leyla is fixing Mahan's collar. He is standing straight and proud in front of her and does not move at all.

"What have you done with our big boy here, Roja?! He looks very handsome."

She throws her scarf on the couch. She is wearing pretty red nail polish. I've never seen her wear nail polish. It looks so good on her pale hands. She says, "Have you seen the beautiful rain pouring down? I didn't want to get home at all. Open that window, Shabaneh."

She doesn't wait for Shabaneh and opens it herself, inhaling the overcast, unpleasant fall weather. The Ahwazi rain-deprived girl that she is, she looks exhilarated.

"Why is your phone off? I called to tell you I could pick you up if you wanted to leave the car for Ramin. I called your landline. Your Mom said you had already left for your tutoring session. Didn't you go?"

"No, they cancelled."

Shabaneh folds Leyla's scarf, sits down next to Mahan, closes the top button of his shirt, and tells Leyla, "Roja didn't bring her party clothes."

"Why not? That's good, actually! Shabaneh, stop messing up his style. What are you doing with his collar? What did you add to the food? It smells amazing. Have you eaten anything, Roja?"

I realize I haven't had lunch, but I don't want to eat. Even thinking of food makes me feel sick today. I ask her, "How was work?"

"It was great! Amir and everyone else at the newsroom are wonderful. Today I had to write two articles. I'm just very tired."

She slumps down on the coach next to Mahan. She seems high on her exhaustion. Mahan says, "Shaba, give me my paintings."

Shabaneh goes to Leyla's room and comes back with a big folder. Mahan opens the folder and spreads his paintings on Leyla's lap. I sit next to them.

"These are so well done, Mahan!"

Leyla looks at the drawings with such love, as if they are her own son's art. Mahan has drawn Leyla in all of them. Leyla with light hair, Leyla in the mountains, Leyla under the skies, Leyla among the trees, Leyla next to a house. She sees them and is overjoyed. Her joy makes me sick; it is so full of sorrow. It's like those happy songs whose lyrics, if you listen to them carefully, are about missing someone and nostalgia and misery, making you want to cry in the middle of dancing. Her joy should have been for her own kid with Misagh, not for Mahan. That's what makes me want to cry. I had wanted to take her home with me. Misagh had just left. Shabaneh and I had stayed with her so that she could put up with the sadness. I don't know how many days we stayed with her, but Shabaneh kept staring at Leyla and at the empty space where Misagh's DVD collection once was and didn't utter a word. At first, I kept talking nonstop. I made plans for Leyla. I didn't tell her that he would come back. Misagh would not come back. I kept saying that we too would be leaving, that we all would leave together. I said, "You take the language test.

I'll take care of the admission and visa." I said, "Why do you want to stay here?" She didn't say a word, just kept staring at me with a dazed look. Then I realized the problem was something else entirely. Leyla didn't even know herself well, let alone know what she wanted for her future to be able to plan for it. I sat down and said, "You could've gone with him. It's not too late. You can still go." She said, "You don't get it. Misagh didn't really want me to go." If I stay here, I'll become like Leyla. Even if everything goes well, and I manage to get myself an apartment and have enough money and love my job and all that, I'll just end up where Leyla is right now. Shabaneh walks out of the kitchen with a spoon in one hand, holding the other hand under the spoon.

"Try this and see if it's good. I'm on a diet for my engagement party. I don't want to overeat."

Why can't I taste anything? "It's good. I should go get dressed."

Leyla puts Mahan's drawings on the floor and follows me. "Let me tell you what to wear."

Shabaneh collects Mahan's drawings from the floor. I don't want Leyla to follow me into the bedroom. She's going to give me a perplexed look and keep searching for clues in my face. Then she'll ask a hundred times what's wrong with me and not let go. Then she'll say, "Be well." Be well? How can I be well? I mean how many days of the week does she herself feel well that she expects me to feel well all the time? She has been at work for just a few days and has gotten distracted. Tomorrow, she'll remember Misagh once again and think about the fact that she has not left and ask herself why she has not left and why Misagh has not stayed and once again she'll feel miserable. Leyla takes out a purple shirt from her drawer.

"I bought this for you from Haft-e Tir Square. I saw it on my way to work the other day and its color made me immediately think of your hair color. I wanted to give it to you when you leave for France to wear it there, but now is a better time. This way I'm going to actually see you wear it."

That chill begins to whirl around in my body once again.

"It's beautiful. Mom also finished knitting my purple sweater today."

"Any updates on your visa? Don't you want to go to the embassy and do a follow-up?"

"No."

I decide to take a leap into the dark.

"Sometimes I start to second-guess myself about leaving. It's much harder than I thought."

"Since when are you looking for easy things in your life? You won't enjoy yourself unless you get your ass kicked by life."

She bites off the shirt tag with her teeth. With her back to me, she says, "You know, Roja, you're almost done with the process, and it might be too late for second thoughts. Your visa will be issued one of these days, and you'll leave, and when you get there it's just going to be you and the joys of your new life. But I think you too, like Misagh, don't really know why you are leaving. This moving away is like taking part in the national entrance exam for college. Everyone took part in it, so we did it too. Like a train was passing by and we all felt rushed to hop up on it with everybody else. I never asked myself why I needed to go to college. If you pause for a moment and be honest with yourself, if you had a good job or someone or something that rooted you in the soil here, you wouldn't really be leaving."

She sits down on the bed and puts the shirt next to her. She says calmly, "Maybe I'm wrong, but for the past few days, I've been thinking that I'm happy that I didn't leave with Misagh."

She looks pale, as if she is terrified of hearing her own voice saying this. I say, "Didn't I say you would feel better after a while?"

"I don't know. Maybe you will be happier later on if you stay too."

"I won't calm down until I leave, Leyla. The thought of it is eating away my brain like a termite. I don't know what will happen there. If I knew, maybe it would be easier for me to just give in and continue to live my life here. Maybe I'm making a mistake. Maybe I'll regret it later. Who knows? Maybe I leave, and then one day I'll wake up in the morning and realize that Iran has become a paradise of nightingales and flowers. Then I would go get a ticket, go to the airport, and come back."

"If you leave, you'll never come back."

She gets up. I should tell Leyla what has happened. I should tell someone, someone other than Misagh, someone who is close by whom I can look in the eye and talk to. It's just one moment. I should tell her. Misagh said, "Tell someone, speak to someone." I open my mouth, but my breath gets stuck in my throat. I can't. I can't tell her. I don't want her to embrace me and say, "You poor darling." The same thing she tells Shabaneh day in and day out. She turns around to look at me from the doorway.

"I'm going to prepare the fruit bowl. Your mom was worried. She said you didn't have lunch. If you feel like it, call her. You can find pants and belts in the last drawer. Take whatever you like."

My words are stuck in my throat. She closes the door. They say humans are capable of anything. They can dry out the seas, move the mountains, or, I don't know, tear down the trees in a jungle. They lie. Humans are not capable of anything. Even if they succeed to dry out a sea, in the end, a group of fucking bastards always comes around to fuck it all up. Then they have to turn around and move away, head toward the jungle, the mountains, or, I don't know, wherever the hell they can, to just get lost and forget that once there was a sea and that they had dried it out. I should look for something, some pleasure in my life. If I find that one pleasure here, I would be able to stay and be at peace.

I wear my new purple shirt and wander around the streets of Toulouse, the ones that run from my apartment to the campus. I walk and feel nostalgic. I'm a stranger there, like the Kurdish man selling watches at the intersection. Not that I won't enjoy my life there, no, but I'll miss it here. I'm not made of stone. Life is hard there. I would be missing everything here, the streets and the heavy traffic and all the fucking mess of this city. I would miss the days I was irritated by Shabaneh. I would even miss my stupid students. I can't be a teacher there; if I'm lucky I could be a server or a dishwasher. I will get exhausted and humiliated. In the evenings, with no money and all alone, I would cry in my room. No one would hear me. Everyone would forget me. My students, my colleagues at work, Ramin, Leyla, and Shabaneh. Leyla and Shabaneh. How long after I leave would they still remember me? A week? A month? Six months? I would end up all alone. Every night in the cold, distressing winter nights of Toulouse, I would email Leyla and Shabaneh. I wouldn't tell them how hard life is. I wouldn't tell them how much I miss them. Even if I told them, they wouldn't believe me. Instead, I would tell them about things that make them laugh. I would tell them that I'm fine, that everything is great. I would say good things about my school and its range of classes. I would tell them about my new job in an elegant office on campus, about my Black and Arab and Filipino classmates. I would only tell them lies. I would end all my sentences with smiley faces. A colon followed by a D, a colon followed by a D. And I would end by asking them to take care of Mom and each other. I would tell them that there is no way the thousands of kilometers between us can separate us from one another. I would be lying. How can it not separate us?

Someone buzzes. Shabaneh opens the door to Leyla's room. It's not just her lips that are smiling; it's all of her face. Excitedly, she says, "Are you ready yet, Roja? Arsalan is here."

"So what? Why are you acting like this? As if he has just returned from a trip to the other side of the world. You just saw him this morning. And then you keep saying, 'I don't know whether I love him.'"

She laughs and leaves the room. I run my hand through my hair and pull it over my forehead. It's grown long. I find a strong pink lipstick in one of Leyla's drawers. I put it on. It smells awfully stale. Her drawer, her vanity, her room, all of Leyla's life is full of old, stale stuff. I throw the lipstick in the trash can and walk out of the bedroom.

Arsalan is sitting on the very red couch where Misagh always used to sit. There are many seats in this house. Why can't he sit somewhere else? With a hand on Mahan's leg, he says something to Leyla that I can't hear. He laughs. Shabaneh puts a glass of tea in front of him and lights every one of the candles she has set up around the apartment. Her fine necklace sparkles on her neck. I say hi. Arsalan gets up.

"How are you, Roja? You're still here?! When will you get your visa?"

"It's none of your business!"

"I want to plan a trip north for the weekend. Will you join us?

"Sure."

I don't step toward him; instead I stand by the kitchen counter and look at the red couch, which doesn't look good under Arsalan's weight. Misagh had been sitting on that very couch. I had brought him some water. His eyes were a narrow, bloody red line. He took a deep puff of his Bahman cigarette. He had switched from the black Kent cigarettes to the blue Bahman ones long ago. He told me, "Do you know why I fell in love with Leyla? You weren't the marrying type. You were wild and restless. I wouldn't be able to handle you. Leyla was a goddess. A goddess carved out of stone, beautiful, calm, elegant. But I can't even handle her anymore."

I open the freezer, looking for Misagh's cigarettes. In their stead, I find some frozen butter. I turn my head toward the living room. Shabaneh moves around Arsalan and the apartment like a woman who has been tending to her husband's needs for thousands of years, bringing him tea and sweets. She secretly glances at Arsalan. They exchange a disgusting smile that makes me want to throw up. Mahan looks at me. He doesn't seem to like what is going on either. I tell him, "Come on, let's go and see what your sister has cooked for us."

Leyla gets up.

"I should go get ready too. Samira will be here any moment."

She winks at me. Mahan follows me. I tell him to sit at the kitchen table. I feel hungry. I open the fridge. It's filled to the brim, like when Misagh was still here. Now that the house is busy, his absence is so palpable. The times I stayed at their place after the parties, he and I would open the fridge door a hundred times during the night and make Leyla call out to us a hundred times, "Leave something for tomorrow. I can't make lunch."

Mahan says, "I want some of these."

I say a long "sure" and bring out the bowl of pasta salad. I grab two plates and spoons and serve us some. I glance at the other side of the counter, where Shabaneh sits next to Arsalan. Are they a good match?

Leyla had been pacing up and down in front of the building of the campus disciplinary committee. She was waiting for Misagh, who had gone in to meet with the head of the committee to stop them from suspending the students who had participated in protests. Leyla said, "I always imagine Misagh being born either laughing or playing around in the bushes. I can't think of him as a naked baby covered in blood, crying and pissing like everyone else."

I was thinking I should've gone in with them. The head of the committee liked me. I only needed to smile at him, and everything would be resolved. Misagh had said, "You don't need to come. We won't take you with us. You don't know how to talk gently with them and you'll just make things worse." That was his excuse. Leyla said, "Misagh is unlike anyone else I've met. Do you think we are a good match?"

I wish I had never said, "Yes, you are." Leyla could have married a quiet man, a quiet man carved out of stone, like herself, a man so grounded he could barely walk, let alone jump around. Mahan has white sauce all around his mouth. I clean it up for him with a napkin.

"Do you like the salad?"

I hear the buzzer. Leyla comes out of her room wearing a long, ruffled navy blue skirt with a yellow shirt. She has gathered her straight light brown hair on top of her head. She looks so beautiful. She has matured so much in the past ten months. Exactly what Misagh wanted. Mature and beautiful and full of sorrow. Mahan gets up and follows Leyla. Leyla opens the door. Samira's son jumps into the apartment like a bird just released. Samira follows him inside. Her eyes move a few times between Shabaneh and Arsalan. She looks more like Leyla than ever. Or maybe Leyla has become more like her since last year, who knows. She says, "Ramin was parking the car. He and Behrang are coming up together."

When she says Ramin's name, I feel as if a miracle has happened. Suddenly I feel like all the scattered pieces of my body are coming together and getting bound together once more. I realize how much I've been yearning for Ramin in the past two days. I lean on the wall by the entrance and wait for him there. Shabaneh arranges some snacks on the table while glancing at Arsalan again. She looks at him as if she has loved him since the beginning of time. Mahan holds Leyla's hand and doesn't let go. Arsalan wants to sit with him. Mahan pushes Arsalan's hand away and gets closer to Leyla. Samira talks about how nice the weather was today and how her friend's child and Arian didn't get along in the park. Behrang walks in and says hi in a strange accent. He keeps bowing and laughing out loud. He looks very European. You can tell that he hasn't been to Iran more than once or twice. He holds the door open and Ramin comes in. His eyes look tired and tufts of his curly hair are all over his forehead. When he hugs me, I feel as if a bucket of cold water is emptied over my heart. As if my heart is Dad's tombstone, and Mom has emptied the water pitcher and the rose-water over it. Perhaps that helped cool Dad down. Like when he got home, and Mom handed me the sweating steel cup full of water and ice cubes to take to him, and my hand burned from the cold of the cup until I reached Dad, handed him the water, and threw myself into his arms. Ramin's arms feel like Dad's, and I don't want to leave them. He says, "What mess are you trying to cover up this time? Your phone has been off since yesterday. Mom said you've been pretty beat up. What's going on?"

My throat hurts. Perhaps it's from not talking. The fucking words are ripping my throat apart. I can't anymore. I mean I can't do it alone anymore. I can't bear it anymore. Up to this part, I could only do it up to this part. It has become very hard, too hard. Like a swimmer, I come up for air. I whisper into his ear, "Don't tell this to anyone, Ramin. Not even Mom."

He rubs my back. The cold water flows down my back and drips over my legs. I whisper in an even lower voice, "My visa application was rejected."

I pull back from his embrace. I don't look at him. I never cry, especially for things that don't matter. Nothing has really happened yet. I'll sit down and think. If I felt like it, I could write the letter of appeal and eventually get my visa. Who said my life is in the hands of these bastards? Only *I* make the decisions. I do, all by myself. Like always. Ramin looks perplexed. He is about to say something. I don't want him to. I hurry to say, "Don't, Ramin. Let's not talk about it. Give me your coat. Do you want some tea?"

I hang Ramin's coat, pick up my purse, and turn my phone on. I should call Mom. She must already be worried sick. Samira is hanging her overcoat. She asks, "Any news from the embassy?"

Fuck. Fuck. Why must everyone know what the fuck I'm planning to do in my life?

"Nothing yet. To tell you the truth, I'm beginning to have second thoughts. I might even decide to stay."

I glance at Ramin. I feel agitated. I don't like that he knows that I'm lying. I wish I hadn't told him anything. Samira laughs.

"Everyone begins to have doubts before leaving. Leyla remembers it well when I was leaving. I wished that my visa would never be issued, and I could just stay here. Then your visa is there, and you get so busy with packing and taking care of everything before leaving that you can't think about any of that anymore."

"But it's taken forever."

"As long as you haven't heard back, you don't need to worry.

With the visas, it might take a week or two more. They just give people a hard time when it comes to the appeal cases."

"A hard time?"

"Yes, the scumbags never respond to letters of appeal. I mean *I've* never seen anyone who's gotten a response."

You're lying, Samira. You're lying. They themselves said, "Write the letter and fax it to us as soon as you can." Why would they do that if they didn't want to respond? You don't really know. How do you even know? You left five years ago. Perhaps things have changed since then. They will definitely respond. How can they not? Arsalan puts his hand on Ramin's shoulder and says, "We can all go up north together. Does this weekend work for you? Are you in too, dear doctor?"

Samira says, "Roja and I will be gone by this weekend. When Roja arrives in France, I won't be alone anymore, so when you all take a trip north, I won't get jealous."

I wish I believed in destiny. Then my life wouldn't be in my own hands anymore and I wouldn't be so sad about it. I would say, "I'm not leaving because Mom didn't want me to," or "I'm not leaving because I was afraid." Or I would even say, "To hell with leaving. It wasn't in the stars. Perhaps it's for my own good that things didn't work out." Ramin holds my arm, and I feel his breath on my face. He says, "You can find another solution, Roja. You've always been able to find a way out. Don't worry."

I had embraced Ramin and said, "Don't worry. We'll figure something out." He was crying. He had a fever. Mom had found out about him working and had slapped him in the face. She had cried and walked out of the house. I had known about it. He had been skipping the last hour of classes for the past month. He borrowed his friend's wheelbarrow and went around Rasht to sell ice pops. He had told me himself but emphasized that I should not tell anyone. He had said, "Who will bring money home if I don't do this?" I didn't have an answer. His history teacher, who had known Dad, came to our house. I had just come back from school. He told Mom that Ramin was skipping classes. I ran into the house. Mom came in. She was trembling. I said, "Ramin is not lost, Mom. Don't worry. He's selling ice pops." Mom hit herself and cried. When Ramin got home, she slapped him in the face. She said, "I can't do this anymore. I'm going to see Mohsen." Then she left the house. Night had fallen, but Mom was not back yet. Ramin was afraid. He was crying. His face felt hot. He said, "How am I going to raise you all by myself?" I said, "I'm a big girl." I said, "Don't worry. Mom's coming back." He said, "She's not." I hugged him. We fell asleep. When we got up, Mom had set the table for breakfast.

Ramin says, "Can you take a few days off from work so that we can go visit Auntie in Rasht while I'm here? She was asking after you."

"First I need to write that letter of appeal, then we can go. And you are right, Ramin. If that doesn't work, I'll apply to go somewhere else. Maybe I'll go to Germany. No, Belgium, Belgium is francophone too, so I might try that. Or maybe even Canada."

"Do what you need to do, and we'll go see Auntie afterward."

I miss Auntie and her wrinkled hands. She's lived her whole life with Grandma, no husband, no kids. It is just her and a bunch of dolls that she washes every day. She has OCD, like Grandma. I have never been of any use to her, but Ramin has been the son she never had. Ramin is everyone's good son. When we were leaving Rasht, she put her head in Ramin's lap and cried. I held her hands in mine and said, "We'll come and visit you all the time."

"Don't go. Tehran is full of snakes. The cars are too fast there."

"Don't worry, dear Auntie. We'll be careful."

"Don't leave. What's wrong with here? Tell your mother not to leave. You'll regret it later."

I didn't tell Mom anything. There was nothing to tell. Auntie was always afraid of everything. I wish we had stayed in Rasht. I could have gone to college there. How long would I have been sad about it? One week? Two weeks? A month? I wouldn't have to go through these days anymore. I've always struggled for useless things. The yearning to get ahead of everyone else in life had driven me mad. Ramin is sitting next to Mahan and they are chatting. Arsalan is frowning. Shabaneh is not around. Perhaps she's in the kitchen. I sit next to Arsalan.

"Dear Arsalan, can you give me your bank account number? I'll repay you the rest of my debt tomorrow."

"I'm not in a rush, Roja. You can give it back later, when you've left and are settled."

"You've been very generous. I have enough money now. And if you hear of any job openings . . ."

My throat hurts. I don't continue with the rest of my sentence and stop right there. It's still too soon to start looking for a new job. I should give myself some time to rest. Arsalan is not paying attention anyway. He's restless. Arian is playing with Mahan and Ramin. Ramin calls me, "Roja, come talk to this kid. See what he's saying. I can't understand him."

I'm not in the mood for children. Samira isn't paying any attention to her son. She's busy talking with Leyla. Behrang looks at her with a foolish smile. You can tell he doesn't understand a word of what she's saying. He only understands "Hello" and "How are you?" in Persian, and only if you pronounce the words slowly and in a measured way. I look at Samira. I want to guess whether she would be happier if she had stayed here or if she is happier now that she's left. I should remember to ask her. Arian keeps shouting, "*Méchant! Méchant!*" He throws Mahan's orange. Mahan gets up and calls Shabaneh. I walk to the kitchen. She's not there. Samira says, "Be a good boy, Arian." Leyla gestures to me to ask whether I've seen Shabaneh. I have not. Arsalan is not on the red couch either. My phone buzzes. It's a strange number. I pick up.

"Roja? Why has your phone been off since yesterday? I was worried. Where are you?"

It's Misagh. I feel short of breath. I feel freezing cold on my back. I look at Leyla. She comes toward me. She might hear his voice. I hang up. Leyla takes Mahan's hand in hers.

"Come on, Mahan. Shabaneh hasn't gone anywhere. She's right here. Roja is going to find her right now."

I look for Shabaneh. I hear Arsalan yelling at the end of the hallway. I open the door to Leyla's bedroom. Shabaneh is sitting on the bed, sobbing. There is a juice stain on her shirt. Arsalan stands over her. I tug at my hair.

"What's up with you two?"

Arsalan tries to shut the door with his hand.

"Go out, Roja. I'll bring her out myself."

"No need. You have no right whatsoever to yell at Shabaneh. Don't you know better? This is not the place to fight. Get out."

He looks hesitant. I grind my teeth.

"I said out!"

He doesn't want to, but he leaves the room anyway. I close the door behind him. I give Shabaneh a tissue. She is gasping for air. I say, "You really should be ashamed of yourself. Is this the time to pick a fight?"

"I don't feel well, Roja. Whatever he says, I burst out crying. He gets angry, I cry. He buys me a necklace, I cry. His mother calls, I cry."

My phone rings again. It's Misagh. Shabaneh sighs, then takes a deep breath and wipes away her tears.

"Go ahead and wash your face. I'll bring you a clean shirt. Hurry up. Get up."

"You know what, Roja? I want to live well, like Leyla. I need to learn. And I'm going to find a way to take care of Mahan, no matter what."

She gets up off the bed. I push her into the bathroom off of Leyla's bedroom. I answer my phone. Misagh's voice is delayed. It comes from far, far away.

"Can you hear me now? Are you okay, Roja? Are you feeling better?"

My throat hurts.

"I'm fine."

"I called you a dozen times. Your phone has been off since yesterday. I was worried sick. What did you do about the visa?"

"Nothing yet."

"Did you send the letter? Did you talk to anyone?"

"No, not yet, but I will. I might even try for somewhere else."

"Where are you now?"

I want to say, "Leyla's and your house," but I can't. My throat hurts again. Misagh talks very fast. He says, "You can do it. It'll get resolved." He says, "I'm sure of it." He says, "Don't worry." He says, "Forget about France. Think about somewhere else. I'll help you out myself." Shabaneh is waiting for me to give her a clean shirt. I open Leyla's closet. Misagh asks, "Are you there? Why don't you say something? Where are you?" I can't believe my eyes. Leyla's closet is full of Misagh's photos. Photos that I've never seen. All in wooden frames of the same size. There are a thousand Misaghs in her closet. All of them join together with the Misagh on the line and say, "Cry, Roja. That'll help you calm down." A thousand Misaghs, in a thousand different places. The first day of college in jeans, the day of Leyla's piano recital in a dress shirt, the day of the strike with a beret, a day at the mountain in sportswear, at the office of the student union, on the trip to Tabriz, on their wedding day, their trips, in bed, at parties. Misagh calls out my name.

"Roja? Can you hear me? Where are you, Roja?"

"At Leyla's and your house. In front of a thousand pictures of you."

My throat hurts. My mouth feels bitter. The pain raises all the way up to my eyes. My nostrils tremble. This is the end. I release my breath. The heat from my breath burns up my face. Drops of warm water find their way through my pressed eyelids, flow over my cheeks, and fall all the way down to my throat.

Photo by Mehri Rahimzadeh

ABOUT THE AUTHOR

Nasim Marashi was born in Tehran, Iran, in 1984. She started her career in journalism in 2007 and became a screenwriter in 2013. She won the Premier Prix in Bayhaqi Story Prize (2014) for the short story "Nakhjir," and the Premier Prix in Tehran Story Prize (2015) for the short story "Rood." Her debut novel, *I'll Be Strong for You* (Cheshmeh Publications, 2015) was selected as the Best Novel of the Year in the 8th Jalal Al-e Ahmad Literary Prize and is in its fortieth printing. The book was translated into Italian and Kurdish and received great acclaim. Marashi's second novel, *Haras* (Cheshmeh Publications, 2016), is in its twentieth printing and has been translated into Turkish and Kurdish. Marashi is the cowriter of the feature film *Avalanche* (2015) and the documentary *20th Circuit Suspects* (2017).

ABOUT THE TRANSLATOR

Poupeh Missaghi is a writer, a translator both into and out of Persian, *Asymptote*'s Iran editor at large, and an educator. She holds a PhD in English and creative writing from the University of Denver, an MA in creative writing from Johns Hopkins University, and an MA in translation studies from Azad University of Tehran, Iran. Her nonfiction, fiction, and translations have appeared in numerous journals, and she has several books of translation published in Iran. Her debut novel, *trans(re)lating house one*, was published by Coffee House Press in February 2020. She is currently a visiting assistant professor in the Department of Writing at the Pratt Institute, Brooklyn.